# Battlefield

रणांगण



VISHRAM BEDEKAR

*Translated by* **Jerry Pinto**

SPEAKING TIGER

SPEAKING TIGER BOOKS LLP
4381/ 4, Ansari Road, Daryaganj
New Delhi 110002

Published in English in paperback by Speaking Tiger Books 2021
Originally published in Marathi as *Ranaangan* in 1939

Translation supported by JSW and Indian Novels Collective



ISBN: 978-81-944908-4-5
eISBN: 978-81-944908-5-2

10 9 8 7 6 5 4 3 2 1



Typeset in Garamond Premier Pro by SÜRYA, New Delhi
Printed at Chaman Enterprises, New Delhi

**Vishwanath Chintamani Bedekar** (1906-1998), who used **Vishram Bedekar** as his professional name, was a prominent and immensely popular Marathi writer, playwright and film-maker. His first and only novel, *Ranaangan*, was published in 1939 and created a sensation in the literary circles of the time. Among the several plays he wrote are *Bramhakumari*, *Naro Va Kunjaro Va*, *Vaje Paul Apule* and *Tilak ani Agarkar*—the last, which investigates the ideological conflict between two friends who were also towering social reformers, is a classic of Marathi theatre. In 1984, he published his autobiography, *Ek Zhaad Ani Don Pakshi* (A Tree and Two Birds), which won the Sahitya Akademi Award the following year. A trained cinematographer, Bedekar also directed over fifteen films, among them, *Thakiche Lagna*, *Satyache Prayog*, *Vasudeo Balwant*, *Ramshastri* and *Pahila Palna* in Marathi; and *Andheri Duniya*, *Talaash*, *Do Bhai*, *Rustom Sohrab* and *Ek Nanhi Munni Ladki Thi* in Hindi.

Vishram Bedekar was married to Malati Bedekar, also a leading Marathi writer and a pioneering feminist.

**Jerry Pinto** is the author of the novels *Murder in Mahim* (2017; winner of the Valley of Words Award and shortlisted for the Crossword Book Award) and *Em and the Big Hoom* (2012; winner of the Hindu Prize and the Crossword Book Award), and the non-fiction book *Helen: The Life and Times of an H-Bomb* (2006; winner of the National Award for the Best Book on Cinema). He has also translated (from Marathi) the autobiographies *Baluta* by Daya Pawar and *Strike a Blow to Change the World* (*Jag Badal Ghaaluni Ghaav*) by Eknath Awad; the memoirs *I Want to Destroy Myself* (*Mala Udhvasta Vhachay*) by Malika Amar Shaikh and *I, the Salt Doll* (*Mee Mithaachi Baahuli*) by Vandana Mishra; Baburao Bagul's classic short-story collection *When I Hid My Caste* (*Jevhaa Mee Jaat Chorli Hoti*); the novels *Cobalt Blue* by Sachin Kundalkar and *Half-Open Windows* (*Khidkya Ardhya Ughadya*) by Ganesh Matkari; and, with Neela Bhagwat, a selection of abhangs by Marathi Warkari women saints, *The Ant Who Swallowed the Sun*.

This translation has been supported by **JSW** and **Indian Novels Collective.**

**About JSW**

At the JSW Group we strive to create, preserve and celebrate the magic of Indian literature. To share the treasure trove of Indian literature with the world, we teamed up with Indian Novels Collective and Speaking Tiger Books to produce English translations of novels from various Indian languages by prominent contemporary translators. We are committed to presenting India to the world through a medium that transcends boundaries and celebrates our invaluable heritage.

**About Indian Novels Collective**

Indian Novels Collective is a not-for-profit network of individuals set up with the objective of bridging the gap between English-language readers across the world and classics of Indian literature by making available quality translations and building reader communities through curated conversations around translations, performances and partnerships that celebrate Indian storytelling.

INDIAN **NOVELS**

COLLECTIVE

www.indiannovelscollective.com

# Battlefield

रणांगण

# One

As far as the eye could see, the carnival of travel. Everyone dressed in their best clothes, faces lit up with the joy of returning home. In every conceivable corner of deck and dock, luggage. Suitcases, cabin trunks, hat boxes, tennis bags—each bag bearing a host of vivid labels, signs of its progress across the world. Boat names, customs clearance labels, cabin numbers, baggage room tags all vie for prominence but the loveliest are those of the hotels. The labels also carry the name of the city to which the bag would go: Berlin, Prague, Amsterdam, Lausanne, London...names as evocative as the pictures on them. Each time we had docked, I had spent some time looking at these labels and enjoying their beauty.

Not today. Today, everyone's in a rush. In such a rush, in fact, that every so often someone bumps into one of the bags but hurtles on, uncaring.

I went to my cabin. The thought of scrambling into my upper berth almost defeated me for a moment but then I got up there and flopped down.

The porthole was by my pillow. Outside, the sky was dark and cast a melancholy pall over everything. The sea was a pit, gleaming dully in the stray rays of sunlight. Carrying uniformed sailors to ships or back to land, the tugboats seemed to be hopping over the crests of the waves, like monkeys on trees. Lifebuoys bobbed among them. On the other side, a lighthouse. In the distance, the horizon began to clear.

Here the ship would turn around. My journey had ended. I was supposed to disembark at Mumbai but my mind follows the ship's route. In two days, Colombo, then Singapore, Manila, Hong Kong and fifteen days from today: Shanghai!

The name makes my hair stand on end. Herta is going to Shanghai. I have reached my destination, but I cannot bring myself to get out of the berth.

~

It isn't just about getting out of this berth. Everyone is delighted to return to Mumbai. Everyone except me. Hindustan is my homeland. I have returned from a fairly long sojourn abroad.

I should be delighted to see my motherland, right?

Wrong.

I am in pain. My whole world has changed. Everything has been turned upside down. After Aden, I had lived in fear of the arrival of Mumbai. In fear and in hope. When a storm was brewing, I would think: if only this would grow, the ship would have to slow down. Our arrival in Mumbai would be delayed a little longer. That's the difference between a land journey and a sea journey. During the latter, you see nothing but water. All around, the same waves, the same horizon. There are no signs that you have advanced at all, however long you've been at sea. So I could keep up the comforting pretence that Mumbai was a long way off. But ships have schedules and while these are not set in stone, they must be met. Our schedule too was met.

We were on the deck together as the ship ruthlessly neared the coast of Hindustan. Herta came close, very close. Her eyes were filled with tears, her voice tremulous with fear.

'Did you see it?' she asked.

'What?'

'Bob, the pilot boat,' she said and now she was crying. 'From the port of Mumbai. It's true. We've reached India. And now you will leave.'

The tears began to fall faster, auguries of a flood to follow.

The ship will be in the harbour for eight hours only. All the Indian travellers have left. Only I remain, prolonging my stay. With barely half an hour left for the ship to put to sea again, I find myself on the dock. Even so, my feet are dragging me backwards. The crowds have begun to thin. By the afternoon, the old passengers have departed and the new passengers are embarking. I pay no heed to them. I stand on the dock for a while, looking around. Cranes are loading freight: grain via the lower decks, luggage from the middle deck. On the top deck, passengers stand, laughing and chatting. Some have been garlanded, others are holding bouquets, everyone is in their best togs. And mixed in is the usual human complement of departure: sepoys, customs officers, policemen, brokers, salesmen.

I had seen all this happen again and again, at each port. Whether it was Naples, Massawa, Port Said, Suez or Aden, the same hubbub.

But on each of those occasions I would be on the deck. This time I was on the dock. Then, Herta would be by my side, taking it all in with a child's fascination, her head swivelling in her eagerness to absorb every new detail. She would pull my arm and say, 'Look Bob, look at that. How odd!'

Today she was in front of me but she could

say nothing. Her tears would not let her. Other travellers were close at hand. A sailor stopped to try his luck with her but she paid him no attention. I couldn't think straight.

Now, I buy a bouquet and give a hamaal an anna to deliver it to Herta on the deck. He is startled but he goes. In my head, I say, 'Herta, little one, my last message.'

I had said as much half an hour earlier. I had extricated myself from her embrace with some difficulty and said, 'Goodbye, friend.' She said sadly, 'Bob, my English isn't up to much. You've polished it up a bit. But just now shouldn't you have said, "Goodbye, my dearest"?'

I took her hand and said, 'When you get to Shanghai, you will understand. Now only friendship remains. Love has been lost. Goodbye, dear little friend.'

And I disembarked.

Do words work? Does even writing this have any purpose? I will never see Herta again. And yet both of us are young. We have our lives ahead of us, our limbs and faculties are intact. Two human beings come together for a brief while, and then they say, 'This is our last meeting.' Does this generally happen? Not much, I would think; except at the time of death. But that is what happened to us.

Now the crowds increase. The gangway is raised. The captain's whistle blows from the deck. The ship's foghorn competes with the seamen's chanting and the great roar of the anchor. The iron pylons by which the ship was bound to the dock begin to be freed and splash into the water. A thousand different sounds come together to produce a clangour that threatens to drown the docks. On top of it all, the band's sweet notes hover. Last messages are shouted, white handkerchiefs flutter a frill of farewell, bouquets are heaved through the air. Tears stand in some eyes and laughter dances in others.

The ship begins to move. I cannot look up. My heart is drowning in the clamour.

Poor Herta.

Poor dear Herta.

~

I lay on the bed. I was not ill. I just could not get up. I lacked the strength. I looked out of the window. Evening. The chowk of the Empire Hotel, the biggest in Mumbai. The same buildings. The same crowds of people. Trams, buses, cars. The same chaos.

I remembered all those other cities: London, Paris, Venice, Naples... I have a friend, Jaggu, who has an odd habit. In the middle of a sentence, he would stop suddenly. 'What are you thinking about, Jaggu?' I'd ask. His voice would be plangent with melancholy. 'You'll laugh but it just occurred to me that it's four o'clock now and I can see the Calcutta Mail steaming into Nagpur. The Delhi Express will be at Jhansi, the Punjab Mail at Delhi, the Frontier Mail at Nagda and oh yes, the Madras Mail will soon leave Solapur.' I would laugh but that didn't stop Jaggu from swooping over the map. At these times, I would think of us flying kites together. That was when Jaggu's imagination would take wing. If we could reach those heights and look down, what an infinite expanse of land we would see, how many countries take in at a glance. Jaggu's mind riding all the Indian trains at once seemed odd then; it seems natural now. Or at least today. For it is evening and I am in Bombay but it must be noon in London. At this time, I would be picking my way through Piccadilly. In another half an hour, it would be time for lunch. I'd leave Shaftesbury Avenue and take a detour through North Regent Street to get to Vine Street and a favourite restaurant. With me, a girl from my college. We did not love each other but enjoyed each other's company. In the middle of Piccadilly is the fountain of Anteros. We would linger on the steps of the fountain as the traffic surged around us and waves of people and cars formed and broke in the circle; all very disciplined though. When the sun came out, a cyclone of colour and beauty would erupt. Even after all these weeks, I could still see the vivid clothes, the beautiful faces and the shapely legs; hear the click of high-laced boots and high heels; smell the aromas of perfume and face powder. These were the highlights of my day.

And Paris? What of Paris? It was the 14th of July, the one hundred and fiftieth anniversary of Bastille Day. When dance music begins to play, the European body begins to move to it, as if by a natural response. Mentioning the 14th of July was like turning on the music. In the streets, in the alleys, in the shops and cafés, Paris couldn't stop dancing. The celebrations had let loose a turbulence of people and laughter and beakers full of the warm South. Beautiful buildings, beautiful young women, beautiful clothes, beautiful streets, beautiful scenes—everything seemed to speak of the best of times. I would recall the heights to which humanity seemed to have risen all over Europe. Naples was the same. And Genoa. People were suddenly frantic in their desire to connect, to live.

All those cities now pass before my eyes. Not Berlin. I have not seen Berlin but that name returns again and again. Herta was from Berlin. I shut off the view of Bombay, return my head to the pillow. When will this wave of pain ebb?

What is this pain about? Herta's love?

Separation from her? I am not a weak man. I have borne the blows of parting before this. I have taken harder knocks. I have watched several small fires burn themselves out. I have poked around in the sad cold ashes and found no sparks. They say the wounds of love are like those inflicted by a tigress: they open their mouths again and again. I bear these wounds on my body but I seem hale and hearty. And yet this new sorrow seems incomparable to anything I have borne before, a near-limitless pain. Will I ever be free of it?

Herta killed herself.

Did I tell you?

I read it in today's *Times*. There's a small section for news from Hong Kong. One of the passengers on the ship I took to get to Mumbai, a Miss Herta von Hinne, jumped into the sea and killed herself. The reporter did not know why. For a moment, I felt only I could know why. And then that certainty faded.

No, I did not know either.

I have been in Mumbai for two days now.

My luggage is untouched. I have met no one. My clothes remain on my body. I sleep in them. I thought I would go out today. Now, I think not. *The Times* is in front of me.

With news from Hong Kong.

News of a suicide.

Another news item in the paper mentions a German householder, Herr Nober. He has been sentenced to three years in jail. A third item concerns the corpse of a German youth, Karl Franz. It was found outside the city in a grove of trees. I knew that name too. Herta had loved Karl once. And Nober was the manager of a German company in which Herta had been assistant manager.

Everything was clear in my head. Those eleven days, everyone's ages, their life stories, their futures...and now Herta's suicide. Another wave of grief ebbed, leaving me numb. The pain was draining my energy as through a wound. When grief bubbles up, there's a moment in which I feel I should mutiny against its dominion, rise up, do something. But what can I do alone? Can the fluttering of a single tree release a tempest?

Writing this is an attempt to lighten that load. But how to write? Where to begin? Where to end? I seem to have begun where I should have ended. But then perhaps, that is as it should be, for my world has been turned upside down. Beginnings and endings, days and dates, everything seems to be disordered. I'm going to try and calm down and tell my story.

# Two

August dawned. The sky was a deep blue, illuminated with the yellow of a rich sunlight. This light cascaded down on to the fields of France, turning them an intense green.

It was around 5 p.m. and the Rome Express had just left Paris. Chakradhar was at the window of a second-class carriage, lost in contemplation of the rural idyll passing outside. He had just spent eight days in the lap of luxury, the effects of which had not worn off yet. He summoned the attendant and ordered champagne. Half an hour later, calmed, he stared unblinking out of the window, bidding farewell to the passing countryside.

The train sprang free of the suburbs. The houses grew smaller. Gaps appeared between them and then the memory of those faded too. Meadows and fields began to pass in a green parade. On the left, a canal ran close to the train, stopped and started, diverted here and there by dams. From a little boat, a fisherman, intent more on the pleasure of pursuit than catching fish, dropped his line and settled down to wait. Light and shadow chased each other over a narrow footpath that ran by the canal. Some young couples dawdled along, in pursuit of each other too.

Everything looked like it belonged in a painting. What dark shadow could fall over this paradise? Then after a tiny station, a row of graves began and as the train ran on, it seemed as if the lines of graves, marching in orderly precision, would not end.

'Is this a very old cemetery?' Chakradhar asked the passenger seated in front of him.

'Old?' the man shook his head. 'That's World War I's gift to France: the graves of all the French soldiers who fell in the war.'

This was the dazzling white winter of death.

On and on they went, mortality memorialized in beautifully engraved stones. They were the remains of a macabre feast Death had thrown twenty-five years ago. Chakradhar felt a chill run down his spine. In an instant a pastoral scene had been turned into a battlefield. Even in this nation of pleasure-seekers, renowned for its love of the good life, the signs of approaching war were visible. Truly, *et in Arcadia ego*.

He did not know French and so he had not been able to read the newspapers in Paris. He had not bothered to get hold of the English newspapers either. It seemed as if every nation was on the boil. He knew nothing about the details though they seemed inescapable. Europe had clawed itself out of a grave only to be teetering on the verge of another. Everyone seemed to believe that war was imminent. But that this should manifest itself here? That seemed odd.

Or perhaps not.

~

One a.m. A club in La Rue de la Mare Blonde. Chakradhar got out of his car. He looked at the dance-hall door where a bunch of young people were huddled in pairs. He took out a cigarette and flicked his lighter but it did not catch.

The night was warm, the street quiet. Then someone spoke, a voice at his elbow.

'Monsieur?'

He turned and saw a woman of indeterminate age. The night has ways of camouflaging a woman's years. But he saw a plump body, rapacious eyes, lips and cheeks hectic with rouge.

'Where are you from?' she asked.

'Egypt,' he replied.

'Egypt? One of the oldest civilizations of the world and you're still alive?' she said and laughed. 'Then you haven't disappeared like all the Indians?'

Chakradhar was surprised. He proffered a cigarette. She took it and said: 'I'm thirsty. Buy me a drinkie, won't you?'

He realized that she was a prostitute.

'Come with me,' he said.

'Long live Egypt,' she replied with a mock toast.

'I don't have much money,' he warned her.

'My union has a fixed rate and I will have to charge you accordingly. But let's get on with it now. We can discuss money later,' she said.

They turned to the car and the lights caught her face. The car door flew open and Chakradhar's driver got out.

'Monsieur, this is mutton dressed as lamb. What do you want with it?'

She pinched him and said, 'Watch your mouth, jackanapes!' He pushed her away and said, 'Get off me. What does anyone want with an old hag? The boss wants a young woman's love.'

She laughed loudly and said, 'More fool him. A war is coming. In two months you might be dead. And where will you find love in these days? Love is for peace time. Love doesn't do too well on battlefields.'

She had Chakradhar's attention now. He said, 'You speak good English.'

'I am English, sir. Casanova says it well. In the game of love you need all the help you can get from all five senses.'

She laughed, got into the car and beckoned Chakradhar. When he got in too, she said, 'Home, James!'

She kept up a steady patter all the way to the hotel in the Latin Quartier to which Chakradhar took her. He opened the door and without a word, switched on the light. He offered her a chair and filled two glasses from the bar. He set one in front of her and asked, 'How long can you stay?'

She took a swig and said, 'For one such as me, every night is a lifetime. Let's say I have devoted this lifetime to you.'

She finished her drink and set the glass down. She took off her hat and turned her back on him. 'Can you help me with these buttons?'

He guided her back to the chair and opened the window, drawing the curtains apart. He stayed there and said, 'I only want to hear your story.'

She threw back her head and laughed. Irritated, he asked: 'Is that so funny?'

She stopped laughing and said, 'You seem

new to this. When a man wants to know what a prostitute's life was like, it's because he's fooling himself. He's telling himself he wants to try and understand himself. And he's even dreaming of a spot of social uplift.'

When she saw that he was annoyed, she said, 'Don't let it worry you. It's because you said "only" that I had to laugh. But you'll have to pay anyway, okay?'

Her coquetry filled him with revulsion. He could see her face clearly now. Her eyes were sunk into her swollen cheeks. There were rolls of fat under her chin. Her lips had been reddened so much that they looked—where had he read this simile?—like a bleeding wound. And between them, her tongue flickered.

Now he felt disgust. He took a hundred-franc note from his pocket and threw it on the bed.

'Get out. Those are your union dues. I was taken in by what you said and brought you here. It wasn't for what you have on offer.'

After a few minutes, she told him her story.

'I was sixteen when the war broke out in

1914. I was still in England at the time but France was one of the vortices of it. Thousands of soldiers flooded the country, all of them preparing to die. Just before each attack, the men would be given a ration of rum. And before they became cannon fodder, they sought the comfort and release of a woman's body. I suppose it was a way to avoid thinking about dying the next day.

'And they were ready to die, poor dears, most of them. They were too young to know better. War was all they knew. War and death. The Germans could not have possibly killed as many people in Belgium as babies were aborted in France. In one year, thousands of illegitimate babies were born. There were thousands of children who did not know their fathers' names. But what of that? The world was exploding around us. No one was in their right minds. Perhaps it would have been strange if it hadn't happened.

'But as long as the wolf was howling at the poor man's door, it was all right. But finally the pack was baying for the rich man's blood too.

Governments began to worry. Soldiers began to be conscripted from the colonies, from allies. Martial law was imposed. But what of that? If a man knows he is on his way to dusty death tomorrow, why should he fear punishment?

'I was in England, working in a hotel as a waitress. I was an orphan, alone, my love away at war. His letters were my only solace. I don't know how we got to France. News began to come in that the French Army was providing feminine solace to the new recruits. All the young women in our hotel were in the trade. And the boats were filled with young women like us. I hadn't been long in France before I entered the trade.

'Queues formed outside our doors. Each large room was divided up into smaller cubicles by curtains. The men were already drunk and could hardly tell what they were doing. They would be in one door and out of the other. When twenty to twenty-five men had been serviced, the girl would leave and another would take her place.

'I feel nothing about it now but it was a strange thing. Sometimes I felt I was doing my bit for the war effort. I was lying back and thinking of England. When the war ended, surely I would be compensated for what I had done for these men. Men? They were boys, really. They were high on patriotism, they were ready to die. Once in a while, I would feel drawn to one of them but there was no time for that.

'And then the war ended. I returned to England but I was now a prostitute. There was no place for me in society, no work to do. Only one job seemed open to me and so I was back on the game.

'In the next two years, I was arrested once. I realized that England was no place for me. There I was an outlaw. I was let off with a light sentence as it was my first offence. But I was quite skilled at my work and so I began again. Once again I was arrested, and once again I went to jail. This happened again and again. When I had youth on my side, I could manage. But when your beauty fades, who cares for you? I began to find it difficult to feed myself. London was no place for me. I thought I might try my luck in a smaller city and so I went to Liverpool.

'And then there was a court case that put the wind up me. You might have read about it in the papers. A Scotsman, out of work and down on his luck, sold the Germans some war secrets for thirty pounds. He had been wounded in the last War, crippled really. He had lived with this disability for twenty years and it had ruined his life. Ultimately, he gave in to the temptation to sell English secrets to the Germans whom he had once fought.

'What frightened me was that the newspapers presented this Scotsman as a traitor. People began to say that he was a Judas. Today, the British seem to hate the Irish. The Germans hate the Jews. Now it seemed to be the turn of the Scots. And I have Scottish roots. This net had been spread for me too. I have committed all the sins possible but I decided I would not commit this one. I could not fail my country.

'And so I came to Paris. Here I can fill my stomach in peace. The law does not harass us.'

~

When a waiter walked down the corridor ringing a small bell and calling, 'Dinner is served,' Chakradhar returned to the present and to the train compartment. It was dark outside now.

The door of the coach opened and an Indian woman entered. She looked puzzled for a moment and then said, 'Sorry, sorry, wrong compartment,' and she turned and left.

Chakradhar got up. The woman had looked very dark-skinned to him. She had painted her lips an unbecoming shade of red. He was reminded of a demoness looking up from a feast of the flesh of children.

Latif came in now. 'Come on, let's have dinner,' he said.

Chakradhar looked at him.

'You're after that dark girl, are you?'

'I'm a pimp. I deal in coal and I deal in gold. But I also eat.'

Abdul Latif was a character. Chakradhar had met him for the first time at Mehta & Co, a sub-brokerage firm in a tenement-like building in a by-lane of East London. He had gone there to meet Mehta before leaving England. He had thought Mehta might accompany him to Paris.

Mehta was climbing the stairs. Chakradhar followed him into his cubbyhole. 'You promised to come with me to Paris,' Chakradhar said even as he opened the door but Mehta hushed him with a gesture. He pointed to Latif who was talking on the phone. Mehta waved Chakradhar to a chair and said softly, 'Hold on. He's on the line to Antwerp. We'll talk later.'

Latif was speaking rapid-fire French on the phone. It was difficult to tell his age. His eyes were black and he had a true Egyptian complexion set off by the fine suit he had on.

When he'd finished, Mehta introduced him and said, 'You wanted company, didn't you? Latif is on his way to Paris. If he feels like it, he might even accompany you to Genoa.'

'Are you returning to India then?' Latif asked.

'Yes,' Mehta said with a laugh. 'He fears war is going to break out.'

'It's all very well for you,' said Chakradhar. 'You're settled. You have a British wife. Your family is here. What's it matter to you if war breaks out or not?'

'Who's tired of living?' Mehta asked, looking at Latif. 'If it comes to that, I'm off to America.'

'You're Germany's Foreign Minister, I take it?'

'Better. Bigger,' said Mehta with a touch of mischief. 'He's an arms dealer. Even if a war isn't imminent, it's in his best interests to cause one.'

Latif lit a cigarette and blew out a stream of smoke.

'You mock me, Mehta. But you're not that far off the mark either. If goods accumulate, they must be sold. If a nation buys arms, it must use them. You cannot tell your people that you have bought so many cannons and so many cannonballs and then let them lie idle. And so to keep profits growing, war must keep going. This is a rule of business. If business fails, profits come down and development goes down. People might even die.'

'Yes,' said Chakradhar. 'It had not occurred to me how we need wars to keep people alive and well. At this rate, the only ones who survive will be the arms dealers and the makers of munitions. And whether this is right or wrong, there is a growing awareness that the military-industrial complex is responsible for the starting and prolonging of wars. The American government has instituted inquiries into the ownership of the arms factories. Britain has a Royal Commission for the same purpose. Many people say these factories should be nationalized. But would that help? The greed for profit is now a universal phenomenon. War is a time when the rich can make some easy money. The profiteers of England and France and their allies and the Jews have left nothing to take from Germany.'

The three of them got up and went to a restaurant. At some point, Mehta said to Chakradhar, 'You'll thank me for finding you such a good companion to Paris. I'll tell you his other trade but that's a total secret, okay? He's into the white slave trade. He sells girls to cabarets, dance houses and brothels. It's not unrelated to his other business.'

The meal ended and coffee was served. Latif

lit a cheroot and said, 'I am very happy. When I was a child, we were very poor. I promised myself I would be rich one day. And now a war is definite. That's all I needed: one war. I'll show the world. I'll be richer than Basil Zaharoff.'*

'Sorry, I haven't heard the name. Who is he?'

Latif laughed. He said, 'There's always some suspicion about the behaviour of arms factories. That British Royal Commission you were talking about? Well, Vickers is the world's largest maker of war goods. Their chief director was one of the witnesses at the commission's hearings. One of the members of the Commission asked, "Do you have any dealings with Basil Zaharoff?" The director used your words, "Sorry, I haven't heard the name. Who is he?" I suddenly thought of that answer.

'But to get back to your question, Sir Basil Zaharoff is one of the world's greatest arms

*Sir Basil Zaharoff (1848–1936) was an arms dealer. *The Smithsonian* calls him the archetypal 'merchant of death—an arms salesman who made a career out of selling to both sides in a conflict.' No one is sure whether he was Jewish or not since he systematically destroyed fifty-eight years of papers and diaries as he sat in his French chateau in his later years.

dealers. He has accumulated a vast fortune. He has a say in almost every country's government. When he starts visiting a country, war is sure to follow. Manchuria, China, Abyssinia, all these wars have been initiated by men like him.'

'I hate this business of war,' said Chakradhar angrily.

'Oh, it's a lovely business. Does the thought of war anger you? Has there been a place in the world without war? Is there peace right now? Just because you don't hear cannon fire, that doesn't mean all's well. My dear fellow, don't fool yourself. All is war under the mask.'

~

Morning at the border. This was the last chance to see those classic French sights: the stands of poplars, the little villages, the voluble, good-looking people. Everyone, Chakradhar thought, from the station master to the policeman had the same simplicity, freedom and loud voices which they accompanied with much shrugging and bursts of laughter. The last chance to hear those frequent '*Pardon monsieur*-s' and those '*Merci mademoiselle*-s' and the other mellifluous sounds of the French language. In half an hour, they had all been left behind. Now the train was passing through Italy, a beautiful land but poorer than France. Nature had blessed the nation richly but the people seemed—to Chakradhar's eyes—backward and old-fashioned.

The train came to a halt at a railway station that nestled by the feet of the snow-capped Alps. A stream ran by it. The houses were neat but old, the people seemed dwarfish. The forests were in full bloom but everywhere there were hoardings with Mussolini's messages. Chakradhar noticed that the people in the street greeted each other with the stiff-armed fascist salute.

In France, he had not understood French. In Italy, he would have the same problem with Italian. But in France, he had somehow felt free. Here his spirit was in fetters. He had begun to feel that way almost as soon as they had crossed the border and come to the first Italian station. It was early in the morning, at five or six. In four hours, they would be at Genoa. In six hours, he'd be on a ship to India. His luggage bore the labels of the ship; nonetheless his bags were checked carefully. He could not understand what the officials said but he detected neither arrogance nor bad behaviour. However, they were clearly suspicious of him. But then his passport was British and relations between the two countries were not amicable.

Wherever he went, the same suspicions, the same signs of impending war. Everywhere Mussolini's messages fulminated: on trees, on houses, on electric poles, in the fields. Just when it was all getting too much, Chakradhar suddenly saw an old man cutting grass in a meadow. He had made a row of sheaves of fodder and was adding methodically to them. As he watched this timeless scene, he could for a moment forget the captains and the kings, the shouting and the cries. But soon, the miasma crept back.

Most of Europe was fair skinned but the Italians were dark, Chakradhar noted. Their hair was black, as ours is. So are their eyes. The

Sicilian women looked like Indian women but he did not feel at home as he had in England or France. The train worked its gingerly way down the Alps to the coast.

Then Genoa.

When Chakradhar climbed the gangway to the ship, it was 2 p.m. The lunch service was over. The ship was set to sail in an hour, not enough time to get off, find a bite to eat and return. Instead he made his way to his cabin, undressed and lay down. Sleep claimed him. When he awoke the ship had left Italian territorial waters. The sea was calm; so was his mind. He looked forward now to ten days of rest. No thinking. No worrying. He would eat, wander about the ship, play some deck games and disembark at Mumbai, laughing all the way.

# Three

The bell rang at teatime. I woke up, my stomach empty. I got out of my berth, washed my face and combed my hair, knotted my tie, slipped into my jacket and left the cabin. It was getting very warm. The bar was hot, crowded and fogged with cigarette smoke as there were no fans.

I went below to the dining room. There was a large table of Indians. Some had already drunk their tea while others were arriving. I pulled out a chair and taking the thin paper napkin from the plate, spread it over my lap. I asked the waiter for tea with milk and sugar.

Someone touched my shoulder. I turned to look. It was a Maratha youth, who seemed to be about twenty-five years old. He smiled and offered his hand. 'Shinde,' he said. 'And you are?'

I liked the look of him. Some faces are like that. You take one look and like them immediately. I introduced myself. Another young man stood behind him. He shook my hand and said, 'I'm Mannan. What's your name?'

He seemed to be a Muslim.

'Chakradhar Vidhwans.'

He frowned a little.

'That's a tongue-twister. How do you spell it?'

Shinde was drinking tea. He laughed out loud and said, 'I'm tired of this spelling nonsense. I hope you're not another German. We were just standing on the deck and one was standing next to us. He wanted to learn English but it was an uphill task for him. Talking to him was death. Whatever you said, he'd stop and say, "Ja? What did you say? How do you spell that? What does it mean?"'

I spread a slice of bread with butter. 'I'm glad you don't like Germans,' I said. 'I have a grudge against them too. At Immigration, I had an argument with one; it left me half-dead.'

Shinde laughed and said, 'There was no way I could stand next to him without him talking. The man was unstoppable. As the ship set sail, I sighed, "Resplendent Genoa!" He said, "What does that mean, 'resplendent'?" Now how is one to explain that? And on top of it, he wanted to know the spelling of practically every other word I used. In half an hour, I was ready to scream. A sailor looked at a girl and said something out of the way. "Impudent brute," I said. Out came his pad and pencil. "Brute? What does that mean?" Now what does one say?'

'What did you say?' I asked, amused.

'I couldn't think of an explanation but he wouldn't let it go either. So I said, "Brute means Italian," and he said, "Italian?" so I said, "And German too."'

Everyone laughed. The clink of forks and spoons had begun to cease. I finished my tea and rose, still thinking about the Germans.

~

The bar was still noisy and crowded. Everyone was making new acquaintances. Groups were forming around the tables. Hindus, Muslims, Blacks, Whites were all shaking hands, sitting down, talking, arguing, squabbling...it was cheerful chaos. Beer glasses clinked, chess pieces were ranged in battle order, draughts games were set up. Eleven days on board. It seems quite interesting when you're thinking about it but when you come down to it, the illusion evaporates. Boredom looms and avoiding it becomes a manic pursuit.

I went to the counter and ordered a packet of cigarettes from the steward and signed for it. I picked my way through the crowd and sat down at a table in a corner where I hoped I might be able to catch some breeze.

I lit a cigarette and looked around. There were about a hundred or so passengers milling about, all dressed in much the same way: jacket and tie. I could pick out the Indians and amused myself by guessing where they came from: a Bengali here, a Punjabi there and a Madrasi. I could not however tell one White person from another. There were some young girls, a few middle-aged people and some elderly faces. The men looked alike. I could not tell what nation they came from or what religion they followed. A young woman was at a table in front of me, also smoking a cigarette. Her eyes were large, her cheeks plump. She was fair with wisps of hair fluttering over her high forehead. I guessed that she might be Polish. A Polish tigress, I thought, a tigress on the prowl. Later I would learn that her name was Marthe.

A young man at the next table said, 'Excuse me, may I have the ash tray?' I pushed it over to him. He was also looking at the young woman. 'A peach, isn't she?' he said with a grin that was half a leer. I was not embarrassed; it is not a feeling you're supposed to have on board a ship. When one goes abroad, one has these strange experiences. In this new space, one has been liberated from the pressure of the expectations of one's relatives and friends. What one cannot say, even to close friends, what one cannot confess—one's sexual desires, for instance—one can blurt out to strangers. Time is short but everyone is aware of that and things get accelerated. It is easy to seduce or to be seduced in this floating capsule of time and space. You can succumb to a fling or a one-night stand and imagine yourself safe from the consequences; you need not trouble to maintain the decencies.

~

He proffered his cigarette case and said in Hindi, 'So what do you think?'

I lit a cigarette. I understood what he meant. He was asking me to assess his chances with the young woman. I answered in the same language, 'What does it matter what I think? Go for it. After all, it's only ten days.'

There was an abundance of comforts to be had on this ten-day trip: eating, drinking, playing, gambling, dancing. There was only one shortage: women. The commonly held view was that one could only assure oneself of a successful trip if one had secured a woman.

The young man laughed and said, 'Bhai, you're truly a philanderer. I can tell your blood runs hot and Punjabi.'

I laughed but did not disabuse him. We began to chat. His name was Madnani, a Sindhi. He asked me whether I liked any of the available girls.

I told him that I had been in Europe for two years with fifteen days in Paris on the way back. All my desires had been satiated, temporarily at least. He shook his head vigorously: 'Bhai, that's impossible. You're an old hand. You stick with me and choose one of them. Let the hunt begin.'

I looked around. Everybody was deeply absorbed in the hunt. There could not have been more than ten or twelve young women. Some were talking animatedly to their neighbours. One was taking the air. Music was playing over the loudspeakers and a few were moving to the rhythm even as they sat. Although there was a certain beauty to this movement and I could see it being fine-tuned with adjustments of the hair and costume, I felt no spark of attraction. Finally, I said, 'Who are they anyway?'

Madnani said, 'Oh, they're all Germans but that's neither here nor there.'

'I have a grudge against the Germans,' I said. 'I'm not going to fall for any of them.'

Not half an hour later, I was with a German.

I was sitting in the bar. Shinde came looking for me. I offered him a cigarette but he refused gracefully. 'I'm sorry, I don't smoke.' He also rejected my offer of supari. So I decided to force the issue.

'I'm bored,' I said. 'Let's find some whisky.'

'I only drink alcohol when I'm ill,' he said.

To hide my surprise, I said, 'So it's not just white women you refuse?'

He laughed and said, 'Vidhwans, I'm a doctor. I have none of the ordinary Indian man's fascination for white skin.'

I didn't think he was lying. There was no need. I had seen any number of Maharashtrian boys in England. The strange thing about them is that they don't misbehave much. I'm not one of them. I had money and a great love of life. What does a love of life mean for a man? It is the adoration of women and I had spent a good deal of time at those Temples of Venus. I said now, 'That's strange. You have no vices and here you are in an atmosphere that seems conducive to the suppression of virtue. And yet you seem to be happy.'

He placed his hands on the table and bent down to say, 'Vidhwans, I see I have made a friend. That's why I'm happy. Shall I introduce you?'

'To whom?'

'A German.'

I raised my brows and said, 'Shinde, I thought that was one thing we had in common: an aversion for Germans. And now you're threatening me with precisely that.'

He took my arm and said, 'This German has a great aversion to learning English. At least, come and take a look.'

Together we left the smoking room.

There were writing tables outside. Two young women were writing letters. By the wall, deck chairs in which a couple of travellers were taking naps. Behind, a ladder. On the left, two large windows. No, French windows. Around us, the

Mediterranean Sea. As the ship cut through the water, sprays rose, decked with foam. A fine mist settled over us. Next to the railing sat a young woman in thin soiled clothes. Her hair was dishevelled and her general appearance spoke of her poverty. A child was trying to climb the rails. His exasperated mother tried to keep him from getting too high up.

Shinde called, 'Louis,' but the boy did not turn around. Meanwhile, I was trying to keep my balance as the waves rose and fell, forming hillocks and then collapsing into troughs. You could feel you were on a swing if you watched them too long and here was a little boy, monkeying about on the rails. Louis's mother saw Shinde and smiled a welcome. She pulled at her son's clothes: 'Louis, *ihr* "uncle".'

Louis was not paying attention but he turned at the word uncle. He had a sweet face but it was clear from his expression that he did not want to talk to this uncle.

'*Nein, nein*,' he said now. '*Deutsch*?'

Shinde turned to look at me.

'See? He doesn't want an English uncle. He wants a German uncle.'

And then he reached over and picked the child up. Louis seemed to like Shinde. He gave him a couple of friendly slaps on the cheek and then nipped him too. He said, '*Onkel, onkel.*'

Shinde, and Louis and I played for an hour. We did not understand what he was saying any more than he understood us. He didn't like English and we had no German.

This barrier only added to the fun. Each time we managed to communicate in gestures and mime, we rejoiced. And each time we failed, we laughed even more loudly. We were all travellers from different lands to different destinations but a child had made children of us all. We didn't talk about the war or other darksome topics. There was no prejudice, no bias in our laughter. We did not insist on this or that nor did we argue and we felt no fatigue. This seemed to spread to the others on the deck and by the railing, as they watched two grown men cavort with a little boy. The memory of those moments brings a pang. And then I wonder whether memory is a blessing or a curse.

By evening, we were both very fond of the boy. Nor would he let us go. It was close to dinner time and I had to change my clothes. I picked Louis up, set him on my hip and went on the deck. Everyone we met along the way stopped to speak to me. The women, who would otherwise ignore us and walk past as if blinkered, now stopped and smiled. Even the Anglo-Indian girl who hated the sight of our brown faces could not resist. We met Marthe who tried to take Louis. She pinched his cheeks gently, tickled him a little and tried every trick in the book but when she tried to pull him away, he simply refused to let go of my neck. Finally Shinde took him from me and I straightened my tie, which had been set askew by our rough-housing. Suddenly someone placed a hand on my shoulder. It was Madnani. He squeezed my arm and said, 'That's the stuff. You catch the child; the child catches the lovelies for you.'

I was a bit sickened but I decided to let it

pass. Shinde was speaking to Louis' mother. She looked happy, the poor thing. The chief steward was close at hand. He was adjusting his bow tie. He winked at me.

'What is it?' I asked.

He came forward. Shinde was talking to Louis. He tickled Louis now and said, 'Good boy. Better Mummy. Clever fellows, you two.'

Shinde went red. He shook his clenched fist in the steward's face. 'Do not say that again or you'll get a taste of this.'

Louis's mother had missed this interchange. She continued smiling as if unaware of the undercurrents.

~

The ship left Genoa harbour. Generally the sea is rough here but it was calm that day and so we neither listed nor rolled. The passengers were in good spirits. Various entertainments were in store but this was only the first day of these festivities and they had not yet begun.

In the bar, my attention was drawn to a four that had been made up for bridge. They had drawn a few other spectators too. One of them was a young woman. She had woolly hair confined by a blue ribbon. She was fair-skinned and had a high forehead. Her eyes were not large but they were a fine shade of blue. Her nose was sharp and straight. Her lips had a peculiar quality: when they met, they turned into a thin line; when they parted, one could see their chiselled curves. Two of her front teeth shone; they were gold.

Who knows if you will be able to conjure her up even after that detailed description? I can see her quite clearly even today. But when I saw her first, I do not think she made any great impression. I felt, I remember, that it was a face with a great sadness lurking somewhere behind her blue eyes. You could see the intelligence in her gaze. I looked at her just as her eyes fell on me. She seemed surprised. She continued to look at me for quite a while until I had to force my eyes away. I was smoking my pipe and pretended that it had gone out and then pretended to be looking for matches.

When I looked up again, my eyes involuntarily sought hers out. The startling thing was that she was still looking at me. Just then Mannan went up to her; it was clear that he had succeeded in striking up an acquaintance for he put his hand on her shoulder and leaned down to say something in her ear. Through this, she continued to look in my direction. My embarrassment evaporated. I took her boldness as a challenge and stared right back.

When Herta and I became friends, I asked her why she had been staring at me like that but she said she was unable to tell. There was no coquetry in her gaze, nor any stealth or hesitation. It was without pretence, as if she did not know what she was doing. Initially it must have been surprise and curiosity; but then it became a kind of greed. What intrigued me was that there was no expression on her face, no trace of a smile on her lips, no flicker of a lash. From what she said, it seemed like it had been her first glimpse of a new love. For my part, I was rather startled, somewhat attracted as well.

Even though I spent a long time looking at her, I did not have the courage to go up and speak with her for a long time. I could not tell whether her look was a welcome or an invitation, an objection or a dismissal. I think that was because of the lost look on her face.

In truth, I was an expert at this game. It had only been two years since my own first love affair had ended badly. I had fallen in love with Uma and she with me. We exchanged the usual promises, swore the usual oaths. The next year, her job took her to Bengal. Her father died there and she was left to fend for herself. We would write letters to each other. From what I remember, I would write from the bottom of my heart and I would tell her of my intense love for her. Her letters were also full of pining. She never expressed any discomfort with our situation or with me. I had money; I had friends, all the comforts and possibilities of being more comfortable. I had what it took to be happy and the fair assurance of making her happy.

And so it was a shock to receive a 'Dear John'

letter one day. I found it difficult to understand, even.

> *The love I had for you was not false then nor is it false now. But living alone proved impossible. I have suffered much in the last few months. I have found another to love me. If you could have seen what I was going through, you would have forgiven me. I am marrying him.*

I could not call her self-serving or cunning. The boy earned less than I did. Nor was he much more educated. But Uma's letter shocked me. At first it was difficult not to hate her. Not just her, I felt sickened by love itself, by its intensities, its intoxications, its very language. Whenever I saw a young woman behaving sweetly with her lover, I would think it a ploy, a stratagem, a trap. Everything about womanhood—its delicacy, its nuances, its subtleties—everything seemed false.

Life became difficult. Finally I took myself off to London. In two years, I developed some expertise in this game of glances. I had money, the desire for the good life and the poison of bitter experience in my veins. Together these meant that while I wanted to have some fun, I was determined to remain aloof. I managed quite well. Now I am not impressed by any of this. I cannot not laugh out loud nor can I weep. The cold air of Europe has frozen my emotions.

But Herta was still looking at me and I at her. I could not will myself to move, to speak even. I was frozen by my own indecision.

The bridge game ended. Mannan returned to Herta's side. He asked her to go with him to the deck. She refused. The talk at the table was about the game. Michael was sitting next to me. He was totting up the points.

'Gentlemen, honours?'

Sahai said, 'Let it go. It couldn't have been more than five or six marks in all.'

Michael shook his head. 'It all adds up. Five marks here, six there, soon it's a hundred. And a hundred marks makes tuppence. Pay or play.'

'Ah Michael,' I said loudly. 'You're worse than a Jew.'

Everyone laughed but I was not paying attention to them. Herta got up abruptly. She grabbed Mannan's hand and went off with him. She stopped at the door and threw me a look.

It was difficult to decipher: disappointment? Anger? Sadness? And then it occurred to me: could it be that she's a Jew?

~

A stout balding German was making his way to my table. I thought he might try to talk to me so I picked up my book and opened it. I even began to read but he was not to be deterred. He sat down and said, 'Good night, sir!'

I looked up. His clothes were ordinary—shorts and a half-sleeved shirt—but his sleek face was that of a Sybarite. He bowed and said again: 'Good night, sir! Nice night.'

He had the look of someone expecting to be liked. It was impossible to disappoint him. I was also slightly amused by the misapplied greeting. I smiled and said, 'Good *evening*, sir. Yes, it is a very *pleasant* night, isn't it?'

His face took on a worried look.

'Good evening, not "good night", is it? I thought one said "good night".'

'You say that when you leave someone. In the evening, you say, "good evening" when you meet someone.'

'Is that so?'

He took out a little book from his shirt pocket and made a note.

'I also said "Nice night". What word did you use?'

'Pleasant.'

'Ah yes. Pleasant. What does it mean? Could you spell it out?'

I was exasperated. I realized why Shinde had got up and left. This was the eager learner of English. I looked out of the porthole. I could only see a circular piece of sky, countless stars and moonlight. The night was truly beautiful, the sky a deep indigo. But this German had no appreciation of its beauty. It was spelling he was after.

He opened his dictionary and said, 'Found it. Pleasant means pleasing. Now what does pleasing mean? Oh dear, I really need an English-German dictionary. Could you please tell me?'

I tried to explain with examples. Finally one of them did the trick. I began to understand his way of speaking and I figured out how to speak to him as well. One had to speak slowly, use easy words in simple sentences and look straight at him. If he did not get a word, worry would crease his brow. I would offer synonyms, other uses, examples, gestures, all to explain the word in question. I offered him a glass of beer. He politely refused. I offered him a cigarette and he refused again with the same courtesy. I began to like him.

Keitel was his name. His laugh was carefree, his speech eager. His eyes seemed happy but there was also compassion in them. It was clear that he had seen a good deal of the world. We talked for a long time. I said, 'If you're on your way to Shanghai, why bother with English? Shouldn't you be learning Chinese?'

'I will need to work in Shanghai. English has value that Chinese doesn't. Do you know anything about Shanghai?'

I did not. 'Even if Chinese has no economic value, won't it help you?'

'Do you speak Chinese?'

I confessed my ignorance.

'I don't think Chinese is a language. You know those toy dogs and cats you get in the market? If you press their heads or squeeze them around the middle, they make some chee-chee choo-choo sounds. That's all I can make out of Chinese.'

He began to laugh and I joined in because he laughed easily and infectiously.

'Your laughter is beautiful,' I said.

He turned serious for a moment.

'Yes, it's as if my throat has been freed now. I had forgotten how to laugh.'

Those words—or was it how he said them?—shocked me deeply. I could not ask about what seemed a private sadness so I changed the subject.

'You might save yourself a lot of trouble if you seek out some dogs and cats,' I said.

'Why me alone? Thousands of Germans are on their way to China. All of us would benefit. Truly.' He added, 'If I could patent the idea, I'd be a wealthy man. I wouldn't have to worry about earning a living or learning English.'

'If you stopped worrying about learning English, I should be delighted,' I said. 'But don't you like English?'

'Hate it.'

'What language do you like then?'

'My mother tongue: German.'

'So why this pother about English?'

'Shanghai has no use for German.'

'Why leave Germany then and go to the trouble of learning English and going to Shanghai?'

'I call myself a German,' he said in a low voice. 'Germany is my motherland. German is my language. But Germany does not acknowledge me as a son. I am a Jew. I have been exiled so I am making my way to Shanghai. I do not know if I will ever see my country again or hear the chaste German of the *Unter der Linden** again, so I have to learn this new language.'

~

So they were all Jews? Illumination came in a flash. This was the key to why they were treated

*One of the most elegant boulevards of all Berlin, Unter der Linden is lined with linden trees that give it its name.

so badly. In this floating world, white people will treat even black people well. They even manage to behave decently with Indians. But not with the Jews. The same was true of the Italians who respect Indians but behave badly with the Jews. Other bits began to fall into place. The German girl who was after Madnani. The girl Mannan had captured. Louis's mother and her affection for Shinde. It all fell into place now. They must be Jews. I had read some bits and bobs about them, lies mixed in with truths. The Nazis had begun to eliminate them. I had read that the same hatred seemed to be spreading through Italy, Hungary and Poland.

On my way to the Grant Medical College in Mumbai, I would pass a Jewish settlement at Nagpada. The people didn't seem to fit with the mental impression I had formed of them: money-grubbing Shylocks with hooked noses, who lacked all humanity. Were these ordinary people, who looked like other Indians, really the repository of all vices, as I had read?

And yet they were also a tribe that had suffered

and borne much persecution. Not an inch of land was left in the whole wide world that they could call home. On the other hand, we were also told that the last World War had dragged on for four years because of their greed. They were accused of having stage-managed the impending war too. Europe, we were told, would burn because of the vindictiveness of the rich Jews. England's enmity with Russia, the possibility of America entering the war, the conflict in Palestine with the Arab Muslims, all this led back to the Jews. They might have no country and no common mother tongue but they numbered many pioneers and thinkers in global culture, a powerful parade from Christ right up to Einstein. So what was their crime? The Nazis said the Jews had broken faith with Germany in the last War. What if the same philosophy of anti-Semitism were to spread to other countries, what then? Would that small band of Nazi fanatics kill millions of Hindus tomorrow? Are Hindu groups and organizations going to kill all the non-Hindus so that none remain within our borders? Is that the goal?

Can that be a goal of any religion? There are so many communities and classes of people who are compradors, people who do not want freedom to come. The foreign rulers protect them today for their own selfish motives. Once this protection is removed, what happens to the sins they commit today? Will they be remembered tomorrow? Or must we simply admit that as time goes on, these volcanoes of hatred will keep erupting? If we're thinking of Nationalism as revenge, if this becomes rooted in our history as a way of thinking, what becomes of man's evolution? I shudder to think.

I was confused. Perhaps the Germans had the right of it. But here was this ordinary Jew standing in front of me. What was his crime? Why was he being punished? Was the need of the nation greater than the needs of the individuals who compose it? This was not a new discussion nor was anti-Semitism a new thing. Jews had been persecuted for centuries. Only this time, it had taken on a new and more ominous form as the Germans turned their efficiency towards the goal of extermination. Would this be repeated in the history of other countries? Muslims had once conquered and then made India their home. Parsis had arrived in India, escaping religious persecution, and after being turned away they had been accepted conditionally. The Nazi philosophy seemed to see the Nation as an Avenging Angel, flaming sword in hand, righting wrongs that might be real or imagined.

Where would it end? Many thoughts and ideas began to contend, none fully formed, none entirely coherent. How does a country become one's country? How many years or generations does it take before a land becomes a motherland? Palestine once belonged to the Jews. Hindustan belongs to the Hindus now. Would all those political certainties remain? Before the Aryans arrived in south India, whose land had it been? Who can claim a language as a mother tongue? The Jews were accused of having ruined Germany but they called themselves Germans, still held on to the language as their own. Was this pragmatic cunning? What did they really feel? What had been their childhood influences?

Shinde arrived with Louis on his shoulders and Louis's mother in tow.

'Good night,' I said to Louis.

'Say "good night" to the nice man,' his mother said.

'*Gute Nacht*,' said Louis immediately.

'No, you scamp,' Shinde reprimanded him fondly. 'Say it in English.'

'*Nein, nein*,' said Louis, shaking his small head firmly. '*Deutsch. Gute Nacht*.'

~

Napoli.

The journey from Genoa to Naples was like a pleasure trip, not even a day long. The Italians must have felt like they were strolling about in their own homes. But for the rest of us, it was all new and exotic. The city was lovely, framed by the terrifying beauty of Mount Vesuvius. It was known for its historic relics. The remains of Pompeii were close at hand. This was also our last time on European soil.

It was about eight in the morning but

already the heat was pouring down on the ship. Breakfast extended up to 9:30, but by 8 or 8:30 most people had hurried through it in order to disembark. Everywhere the only conversations were about when we would get to go ashore.

I went below. The dining room was almost deserted; only ten or fifteen people were finishing their tea. Keitel was sitting at a table in a corner. There was another Jewish couple and an elderly woman who had the look of a missionary. The couple saw me and smiled. I drew up a chair and picked up a menu.

Herta came up with her mother. Mannan was with them. Herta's clothes were the same ones she had been wearing last night. I assumed that she must be quite poor. I remembered our last encounter, how she had left angrily and not returned. I had got her wrong. I did not think she was the kind of woman who would try her luck with men, but I could be wrong. I ordered porridge and settled down to wait for it, my napkin over my lap.

Everyone else was finishing breakfast and

discussing the inevitable: their plans for Naples. Waiters came and went, bringing bread and jam, but ten minutes later there was no sign of my porridge.

I looked at the waiter as he passed me by for the nth time. He was a fit young man with an arrogant face. He approached and poured some tea for another passenger, ignoring me again.

'You do remember my porridge?' I asked.

'Yes.'

'See to it then,' I said, my voice rising a little. He came back and bending his head, said, 'Go sit at that table.'

I was about to ask why when he added, 'This table is reserved for white people. Blacks like you are over there.'

I shot up from the table and grabbed him by the shirtfront and shook him. The tea things began to rattle in his grasp and everyone looked up at us.

'Oh Maria,' he mumbled.

'You swine,' I said, 'Say that again and you'll be licking the floor. Get my porridge here and be quick about it.'

Suddenly a whole bunch of people was at my side. Mannan came over as did some other waiters. The head waiter came to apologize. The Jews looked on, bemused. In a little while things quieted down and the service started again.

I would not have been surprised at such a thing happening in England. At least they have the right to be racist—if ever there can be such a right—conferred upon them by their economic and political might. But the Italians are the beggars of Europe. They have the darkest skins too! They will trade with Hindustan but they are arrogant enough to believe that they are superior to us and can behave badly with us. My blood boiled at the thought.

I suddenly realized that everyone was looking at me. I kept my gaze lowered but I couldn't eat. I began to recover only when the table emptied. Finally I looked up. Herta was looking at me with something like respect.

Breakfast ended. I took out my pipe and tried to light up. Match after match went out, extinguished by the ventilator which, I did not realize then, was directly overhead. It didn't help that my hands were shaking. Finally, Herta laughed, got up, and swung the ventilator away. The next match took.

I looked up at her. She had a cigarette, unlit in her mouth. I lit it and thanked her. Her smile held a trace of satisfaction in it. When I lit my pipe, I noticed that my hands had stopped shaking.

~

Naples was very beautiful. I had spent the previous winter there but then snow had swathed the city, covering its natural beauty in a white veil. The edges of the familiar had been blurred; forest, farm and farmhouse had all been submerged. The trees had been polled, their branches stumps that bore the snow with stoic resignation. The endless white had turned it into a cathedral, bathed in a deep winter silence. All of creation, the living and the non-living alike, seemed to be hushed, expectant, as if anticipating the miracle of rebirth.

Summer had wrought that miracle. Today, a benevolent sun was pouring light and heat down upon the city. And Naples was beautiful in another way now, basking in the sun.

There were five of us in the car—Herta, Shinde, the Hermann couple, me—not to mention the guide. I had shorts on. Herta was in the same clothes. When the car turned, she would lose her balance. At first she held on to the front seat to keep herself steady. From time to time, she would brush against my bare knees. She tried to avoid such contact at the beginning. When we were returning, she gave up the struggle and simply held on to my knee. At times, she would lean on me but seemed to be in no hurry to return to her place. It was very hot. In the deep shade of the trees, tourists lolled at their ease. The streets were crowded and narrow. Old tramcars, vegetable-laden handcarts, the noise of the market, the dilapidated houses in the foreground, the small shops, and from them the professional patter of dozens of guides—I should have been taking all this in but the only thing I was aware of was Herta's body touching mine.

The upward climb ended. We stopped at a small establishment. Its door was small, the windows picked out in lime, the brickwork exposed. For some reason, it brought to mind the rib cage of someone afflicted by tuberculosis.

We went in. It was a restaurant. We crossed the middle room and went out on to the terrace. Tables and chairs were ranged about under a bright and cheerful awning. From this terrace, all of Naples was spread out in front of one. Excited, we went to the very edge to look down.

From the sea to the mountains, grand houses had been built. The sky was busy with clouds. And above it, Mount Vesuvius' peak, a noble and revolutionary idea for an epic set in quotidian reality. It was misted in fog and snow. Below it, modern Italy was exhibiting its power. There were workers and workshops, aeroplanes taking off and stevedores unloading cargo. Nothing seemed to affect the quiet of the shrines set on islands out in the bay; or the summer-houses in the gardens. Italy teemed with life, all of it seemingly unaffected by the unequalled natural beauty, which surrounded it. Plato had dreamed of a philosopher king, a man of learning and of wisdom and one skilled in athletics too, who might provide enlightened rule. I felt Naples might be the right setting for such a one as he. But then my philosophical cogitations were squashed as the hobnailed boots of a walker might a wildflower, when we were informed that we must pay or play. This was a restaurant and if we wished to linger and think about water shrines and Platonic ideals, we must order some refreshments, something to drink, perhaps? Herta and the Hermanns said that the car hire had exhausted their budgets and could not spend any more. Shinde and I did not feel it right to linger without them.

In the car, Herta covered her eyes with a grubby handkerchief.

'Look at the shops, young lady,' said Frau Hermann. 'Take a good look. Who knows whether you'll ever see this again? See how lovely they are.'

'I might want to buy if I look,' said Herta. 'And that will be tormenting. Better not to look at all.'

~

I was leaning on the railing, chin in hand. My face was wet with spray. The lights of the ship were shining in the water. I watched, fascinated, as the ship cut through the waves, sending water up to catch the light for a moment before it fell back into darkness again.

In the middle of the deck, there was a small rail placed crosswise. The area towards the prow, on the other side of it, was empty. It was forbidden to passengers. Here, coils of thick rope lay in heaps, there were huge iron chains and small cranes to raise and lower the anchor. Then the prow with the flagpole on it. In the middle of all this was a small iron curved bar from which a huge bell was suspended.

One or two sailors were sitting on the coils of rope, smoking cigarillos. A few passengers were also on the deck but it was difficult to tell who they were in the gloom. In a dark corner, a young couple clung to each other: it was the Anglo-Indian girl and a white man. I averted my eyes and so I did not notice when Herta arrived to stand by the railing. When I turned my head, she said, 'It's me.'

I laughed. 'Yes. I was about to say that I had seen you but that wouldn't be quite true. It's difficult to see in the darkness.'

'Is that so?' she asked, without turning her eyes from the sea. 'I could say I hadn't seen you in the darkness because you are dark.'

'I may be dark but not as dark as your hair. When your face is covered with it, how would anyone be able to tell it's you?'

She looked at me and was about to reply when an errant wave sprang up and splashed her face. She had a thin coat draped over her shoulders. She drew it around herself with one hand and asked, 'Sorry, may I?' and reached for the handkerchief I was holding.

'I've used that,' I said. 'Let me get you another.'

'Why?'

'I've been using this one.'

'Never mind, it can't be dirtier than mine. You must have just started using it today, right?'

'Yes.'

'Then it will be fine. I've been using mine for two days now.'

I took the neatly folded handkerchief from my coat-pocket and gave it to her. She wiped her face and pushed the hair that was sticking to her forehead and cheeks back. I said, 'Not to be rude or anything but why use the same handkerchief for two or three days?'

'Handkerchiefs are the least of my problems. I've been wearing the same clothes for the last three days.'

'I did notice.'

'They can't find my luggage.'

'What?'

'Yes. They say that my bags must be on board but they can't lay their hands on them.'

'How can that be? They must be in the baggage room. Have you checked with the steward? Come on, let's find him.'

She laughed at my enthusiasm. I remember her eyes shining at me as I approached her, ready to play the Knight Errant of the Lost Luggage Claims. Naturally, she had already asked the steward. They had together searched the baggage room, up and down, in and out. They had then expanded the search to the other cabins, but no sign of the bags. Nothing was left: their clothes, the books they had managed to pack, the cosmetics they had allowed themselves, her mother's medicines...all gone.

I couldn't believe it. The journey to Shanghai would last several weeks and through it all she would have to wear the same clothes, wipe her face with the same kerchief. What state must the old lady be in? Such a beautiful girl to be deprived of her clothes in this way. I proffered my handkerchief and said, 'Keep it. It's new.'

She shook her head: 'No, no, I'm sure they'll find my luggage by tomorrow.'

I insisted but she refused again. She pointed past me and changed the subject.

'Is that a star or a light, friend?' she asked.

I looked at the speck. It was difficult to tell.

'A star, I think,' I said.

She shook her head. 'No, I think you've got it wrong.'

The excitement of contention got into me.

'It is a star. Let's bet on it.'

She sighed. 'Must you talk about money? I thought you'd know how poor I am now. I did tell you, didn't I?'

I was silent. I was shamed by my own insensitivity and the frank ease with which she spoke of her predicament, as if it were an ordinary fact not worth concealing. She was looking around.

'Such a beautiful night and you want to make bets. You would find it difficult to love.'

'Love?' I said with a short laugh. 'Who knows whether I can love or not. But do you think I'd make some poor unsuspecting woman a good husband?'

We crossed the railing and went on to the deck. The speed of the ship began to increase. The breeze freshened and the seas began to swell.

The deck and railings were wet. The breeze caught at her clothes and whipped her hair around her face. Her overcoat, thrown over her shoulders, also billowed.

'Put it on properly,' I said. 'That will be less of a bother.'

'I can't,' she said. 'It belongs to Frau Hermann. My shoulders are a little broader than hers and I don't want to tear it.'

We stood by the rail. She secured the coat by standing with her back to the rail and pressing against it. I wiped the rail with my handkerchief and leaned my elbows on it.

An endless quiet but without the fear of loneliness, broken only by the sound of the ship's engines and the slap of waves and then even those faded away as one grew accustomed to them. The sea looked like some primeval monster, stretching lazily, each wave an ancient muscle flexing. It had engulfed the horizon, this monster, whose breath was fresh and green. We did not even look at each other. We said nothing as if aware that this quiet was precious; that strange things may grow in sea-green silences. Herta moved a little closer and I looked at her now. She turned her gaze on me. Her eyes were filled with warmth. Her coat sleeve, empty, wind-filled, reached out to me, a spectral arm flapping against my shoulder. I took hold of it and anchored it to the rail.

'I should be holding your hand,' I said, trying for the right tone and failing, 'but I'll make do with your sleeve.'

'To be happy with the minimum may be acceptable to some, not to me,' she said and turned again to the sea.

I let go of her sleeve and took her hand and pressed her fingers. Still looking out to sea, she said, 'Don't forget we haven't even been introduced. My name is Herta.'

'My name is Chakradhar Vidhwans.'

'*Mein Gott*! I don't know how we can be friends when you have such a mouthful of a name.'

'I'm sorry,' I said. 'My mother had no idea that I should meet you one day when she chose my name.'

'But could she have used that tongue-twister all the time? When she was being affectionate? Surely you had a pet name?'

'Well, everyone at home called me Babu.'

'Bob?' she said and before I could correct her she was announcing, 'That is what I shall call you: Bob. Or if it comes to that, Mr Bob.'

'As you wish,' I said with a smile. 'But Mr Bob might work until we get to know each other a little better.'

'Mr Bob?' she tried the sound of it. 'No. Not for me. Bob will do fine. Bob. Right, Bob?'

Her hand was in mine. I pressed it and said, 'Yes, Herta.'

~

When a beautiful dream ends, a cloud of depression descends. I slept and pleasant images danced before my eyes. I sought them out again and again. Because of these intoxicating dreams, I did not know when I fell asleep.

When I woke up, it was nine o'clock. Breakfast time was over. My body was lethargic but my mind was fresh. I called the steward and ordered tea in my cabin and lay down in my berth and looked out of the porthole.

Memories of the previous night came flooding back. Through that voyage, I began a strange habit. I began to go over what had happened to me, examining it in memory as if I were a stranger to my own experiences, watching from another perspective. I would try and recall the situation and how things had happened, how the characters involved might behave when the situation ended and they were alone again, what their emotions might be. I would try and relive the whole thing from a multiplicity of viewpoints.

There was no shortage of scenes to imagine. Each day brought fresh sights, new experiences, more acquaintances and therefore more subjective standpoints from which to view what was happening.

I began to think about Herta. What about Herta? We could not have spent more than eight watches in each other's company. For much of that time, we had not spoken to each other. And though I thought of myself as a man of the world, this morning I was getting gooseflesh just thinking about the previous night. Was this still my body? It felt lifeless like a sitar in its cover, its strings slack. It felt dirty too, with the soiled clothes of the night before. There was not a pore in my body that had not experienced love, true or store-bought. My lips had been smeared with kisses of all kinds, sacred and profane. My eyes had taken in the blues of many seas, had tried to investigate the depths of many so-called 'unfathomable eyes'. Had someone told me last night that the very next morning, I should find myself fresh and awakened to all sorts of possibilities, I would have refused to believe it. I would have called him a fool and thought him inexperienced but it was the other way round. I felt now as if I had never had any experiences before. A new energy had been born in me.

Had I fallen in love with Herta last night? That might explain the erasure of all the others who had gone before. My body was alive again, my spirit awakened. I had no idea whether a snake sheds its skin when it moults or whether it moults only when its new skin is ready. But last night had catalyzed a sloughing. All ifs and buts had been erased. I replayed the moment.

'That couple standing behind us?' she said.

I turned to look but she took hold of my chin and turned my face away.

'What is it?' I asked.

'Don't look, Bob,' she said. 'They're lost in each other. You'll embarrass them.'

'What do you mean "lost in each other"?'

She took me by the shoulders now. I turned to her. The railing behind her framed the sea. From the corner of my eye, I could see the young man and woman. The young man had the woman pressed to his chest. As for her, she had yielded to his ardent kisses, her body bent as a bow is bent by an archer.

Above, a small bell rang in the captain's cabin. For a moment, a searchlight lit up the darkness. The contours of their fused form were suddenly illuminated. The stars behind them were erased.

Then again it was dark and the sea returned and the sky returned and the dim light of the stars began to come back, one by one.

'Now let's not talk about them anymore,' she said and turned her face up to mine.

Her uninhibitedness surprised me. I drew her close. I smoothed the hair off her forehead and kissed her. We stood like that for so long that we did not notice when the coat slipped off her shoulders. Then as the wind blew a little colder, she clung to me and said, 'Bob, it's getting chilly. Hold me.'

~

It's not that I remember that kiss because it was my first. Nor was it hers. Neither of us could rank it in a sequence of kisses we had enjoyed.

Now it seems odd. My lips were as impure as a glass tumbler in a restaurant. But this kiss was different. It had none of the show of decency, the stealthy fumblings of the kisses in a Hindi film. Nor was there any vampirish eagerness to consume, to draw from, to suck dry. Once the emotional storm of the encounter had spent itself, one could surrender to an intense peace. It was straightforward, simple, innocent, uninhibited. There was a challenge yes, and unsatisfied longings too. She clung to me, recognizing the oddness, the intensity of this moment. Her breasts were heaving, her breath coming in pants. She pressed her hand against her ribcage and sighed suddenly, 'This is so sudden, so soon. Is this an infatuation? Whatever it is, you'll have to handle it. I can't.'

We began to approach Messina Bay. The ship slowed down. We now had our last glimpses of Italy at Reggio. On either side, a garland of lights, high on the cliffs, the signs of habitation thereon. The water was now calm and reflected the lights.

On the right, Sicily. In front of us, a lighthouse, its beam sweeping the waters. It would light us up for moments and then pass by and drop us back into darkness. Another ship crossed our stern; its lights disrupted the darkness, caught the foam on the water.

Herta was watching this chiaroscuro, fascinated.

'Bob, is this the limit of human happiness? It was only two days ago that I left a life of persecution and horror in Germany. I had turned into my own grave; now I feel exhumed, reborn into light and fresh air.'

I was startled but then I realized she was not in control of herself. The ship drew close to Messina. The beam of the lighthouse caught us both and the flecks of brine on our faces sparkled. Her hair, caught by the breeze, teased my face. Her lids were heavy, stray curls clung to her forehead. Her nostrils were flared, her lips taut with desire. She took my arm and put it around her waist. The lighthouse beam caught us at just that moment.

'What are you doing, Herta?' I asked. 'There are people around. Someone will see us.'

She moved my hand away and swung around to face me.

'Do I care what people think?' she demanded. 'You're saying I should throw away such happiness as I have found for the sake of people? Never. Let the world come for me. I'll shout my love in their faces. I've borne a lifetime of grief. And now the world wants to judge me in these moments of happiness?'

Her voice began to rise. I laid a soothing hand on her shoulder.

'Herta,' I began but she shook her head determinedly and said, 'Bob, if you can't bear to see me happy, you have only to say so. You do want me to be happy, don't you? Then I fear no one. Let what will happen. That bell over there? I'm going to ring it. I'll shout it from the rooftops: I am happy. We're happy, both of us, happy, happy, happy.'

I could only stare at her. Then my attention was drawn to the bell. She too began to look and started to laugh.

'Why are you laughing?' I asked.

'I suddenly remembered that church bells are tolled to announce the joy of marriage. I see now how deep these roots go.'

~

The steward came in to clear up the cabin as I lay in my berth, replaying all this. The dustbins were cleared, the shoes were taken away to be polished, the used towels were replaced with clean ones. As the steward left, he said, 'You've gotten into the habit of staying up until all hours and then lazing about in bed all morning. It will soon be time for lunch.'

He left and I sat up. Outside, the daily routine of the ship was in full swing. I got up and put on my dressing gown. As I shaved in front of the mirror, Herta continued to plague me. The sweet nothings of the night seemed hollow and inconsequential in the harsh light of day. All my *affaires de coeur* came crowding back. Uma had been the first. After that, they had all been the same. Why had I sought out those women? The thrill of the chase or the delight in the victory? A relentless cycle of desire and satisfaction, fresh desire and satisfaction. Is this worth anything? Had that been love at all? And now?

Herta might be in love but what about me? Was there any point in her loving me? Yesterday, we did not know each other. Today, there is no distance between us. And yet we are only fellow-travellers, brought together by chance. What trust could I have in her? But what was the need for trust? If she were up for a few larks, then I was good at making such encounters pleasurable. Short acquaintances, momentary friendships, temporary loves. Once we part, the day is reborn, the night is done. Not the first time for me, nor the last, perhaps.

Day after tomorrow, we would be at Port Said. In a week, Mumbai. And after that, she would go into the basket of fading memories into which I had tossed the other girls' names along with their love letters and notes.

Why bother about all this? The night had been beautiful, but then there had been many such nights in Paris. What does the beauty of the night count for in broad daylight?

I washed my shaving brush and cleaned my razor. I splashed my face and dried it. I creamed my face. To bathe, one had to step out of one's cabin. As I combed my dishevelled hair, I caught sight of my face in the mirror. The signs of prosperity were upon my face, along with the fullness of youth. My hair was silky and soft. On my lips, the traces of a life of lust. My chin was sharp, my face had character, even if I said it myself. Uma often said, 'When I first saw you, it was as if you settled into my heart. But there was also some kind of fear.' That must have been a fear of love repressed. And suddenly a thought came to me. I knew how Uma had responded. Other women had also been drawn to my looks. So how could I be sure that Herta wasn't just having a little fling? Poor thing. She might have fallen prey to the same fascination. And if she had, what of it? History might repeat itself. It was true that Herta had not said she felt any fear at seeing my face but she had admitted her feelings, hadn't she? So why was I assuming they were fake?

I felt confused. I patted the last recalcitrant hair into place, thrust my feet into my slippers, picked up my towel, sponge and other bath paraphernalia and went into the bathroom. I turned on the hot and cold taps, fiddling until I achieved the lukewarm temperature I prefer.

Then I sat down and watched the tub fill as I smoked a thoughtful cigarette.

Perhaps Herta was in love. What of that? She was an adult and she would have to deal with her feelings. I would warn her that we could not marry. I would get down at Mumbai and be free. And who knew what would happen next? I had no faith in the constancy of women. When women play the game of love, they may collapse but they can come back to life, again and again. I had no business worrying about her. Today we would laugh a little, dance a little, play a little and tomorrow, weep a little. By Colombo, she would have found someone else. That line from Uma's letter kept coming back: 'The love I felt for you was never false nor is it false now. But I have found someone else to love me. I know how much I have suffered. If you could have seen my suffering, you would have forgiven me.'

'Suffering?' I remember thinking to myself. 'You gave a fair imitation of a woman in love. Now don't put on your suffering-woman act.' Do women really suffer? I had once read a thesis by a German psychologist. He was of the opinion that the female of the species, far from being full of gentle feeling, is fundamentally cruel, hard-hearted, ruthless. That is why women make the best nurses. They can bear to nurse the ill, the wounded, the convalescent. In the opinion of the good doctor, men cannot bear these sights as they are the gentler sex.

Maybe Herta would love me and lose me but she would not die of it. What about me? I had to admit it to myself. After Uma, I had not experienced anything other than superficial friendships. This seemed different, genuine. But then what did I know of Herta's true nature? Was I going to get entangled again? My experiences should have made me immune. When you need a drink, you go and get one and you're rejuvenated. Which hotel you drink in does not matter. The desire for the company of women is well and good but it does not depend on the specific woman. Had it been the Polish girl instead of Herta, there would have been no difference. I kept testing this supposition inside my head.

Was it true? Could it be true? But in truth, I had made up my mind. I could look after myself. Herta must look after herself too. I could not take responsibility for her. The cigarette ended and I began my bath.

~

No one could tell for certain what time we would dock at Port Said. Then someone said: 2 a.m. It had been the general opinion that a well-behaved ship would arrive at around 10 a.m. for this would allow everyone to buy what they needed, post letters, send telegrams or just wander around. The seasoned travellers had already formed groups with the idea of going into the Arab Town to have fun. Every port is home to some travellers and some sailors but Port Said had taken on the air of a stately pleasure dome.

The 2 a.m. schedule came as a shock but it did not quell the excitement. Everyone was suffering from cabin fever. Solid ground would let us all stretch our legs again.

Afternoon tea taken, the passengers made their way to the deck. A steward arrived, the one in charge of notices, announcements and such newspapers as made their way on board. He opened the glass pane behind which hung a map. On this map, a pin would show exactly where the ship had reached. Each day, he would remove the previous day's pin and after consulting a slip of paper on which our latitude and longitude were noted he would affix it again.

A group gathered around, mainly Jews. I was sitting on a deck-chair by the bulkhead. I thought I'd have a look at the map after the crowds had dissipated a little. I saw Keitel measuring the distance between the pin and the port. He said, 'It should be midnight or one o'clock by the time we get there.'

The rest wandered away but Keitel remained there, staring intently at the map. I got up and went to stand behind him. He had a pencil in his hand and he was taking it for a walk across the world. He was tracing the sea routes, the air routes, the rivers—in what seemed like a random excursion. I had often seen him there.

'What are you looking at?' I asked now.

He was startled. He turned to me and said, 'I'm looking at our route.'

'You're looking at the ports of Africa, the rivers of Arabia, the cities of Hindustan, the hills of China, the railways that link them all. Those aren't on our route.'

'True,' he said with a little laugh. 'But I haven't looked at Europe. You've seen me here, every day, haven't you? Like me, many people are staring at maps. Each new country, each new port, each new city, evokes a new dream. Can I go there? Would I be able to feed myself? Would I find somewhere to settle?'

I knew that it would all boil down to the same story. 'Everyone else looks at the map and probably thinks: how limitless the world is. It isn't as if you lose your freedom if you leave a country. You can go anywhere, live anywhere.'

As we spoke, we gravitated to the deck chairs. Marthe's mother was close by. I smiled and said, 'Have you been studying the map too? Which country would you like to live in?'

Keitel translated my question and her reply: 'What difference does my liking make? I'll live anywhere I'm allowed to live.'

'Why talk like that?' I asked. 'Look at the map. So many colours, each representing a different country. Look how little is painted in the Nazi colours. You can live anywhere you want. There are other nations, richer, more beautiful, better than Germany. You can take your pick. Look at the map and choose and I'll get you there.'

Keitel laughed. 'I have thoughts like that too,' he said. 'But the worries follow. The questions begin to surface. They're small problems but then they mount up and life begins to seem impossible. Take Egypt. I thought I might be able to live there but the heat frightens me. Hindustan is like that too. I've heard of cities like Lahore and Delhi but there too I've heard it can get very hot. Almost too hot to live.'

I said, 'What's to fear? It gets to a hundred and ten degrees in the shade in my village in the summer and I'm alive.'

'Christ!' he gasped. 'A hundred and ten in the shade!'

The woman shuddered in horror. Keitel added. 'A sailor was saying this morning that the sun is very hot over the Red Sea and the deserts around it. Even the breeze can burn you, he was saying. Do you think he's got it right?'

He actually looked a little scared.

'Nothing of the kind,' I said dismissively. 'Don't worry for nothing. Don't Europeans have settlements in Africa?'

'True,' he said. 'But each one presents its own problems. If you're young, you can manage. Take Herta's mother; can she, at her age, live in a hot country, I wonder? Let's say we get off at Port Said or Aden. The clothes we have are all meant for cold weather. Tropical weather means buying new clothes. Where's the money to come from?'

Suddenly he had made it real for me: how much a refugee must deal with, what he must consider when deciding on a new life. Truly, it was not as easy as I had thought. To settle down somewhere, to worry, to live in poverty...

To give him some confidence, I said, 'Baseless fears. Not every country lies in the tropics.'

'I know,' he said. 'So I'm looking for a village

in the mountains, with a river running through it. I try to imagine what the breeze will smell like. We're on our way to Shanghai, nein? I have its geography down pat.'

Behind us, we could hear Marthe and her mother come up. They had been having a row. Marthe wanted to go to Port Said with Madnani. They had planned to hire a car and motor down to Cairo and catch up with the ship at Suez. The old lady did not approve of the plan. Finally, Marthe had announced, 'I'm going anyway,' and marched off.

I turned to Keitel: 'Going to Port Said tonight?'

'Not sure,' he said.

'Don't be silly. Palestine isn't that far. You might want to try it for a while.'

At the mention of Palestine, Marthe's mother looked up.

'You asked where I'd like to settle. I'm sick of the entire world. I just want to die and have my bones gathered to my ancestors in Palestine's holy land,' she said.

~

Louis kept me amused. His mischief sometimes seemed to have a deeper meaning than one might expect from a child. Were he a little older, one might have even suspected him of irony. Shinde saw him as a clown who held up the mirror to European mores. He would say, 'Good morning, Louis,' and offer a hand to shake. Louis would have none of this. He would raise his arm in a Nazi salute but it always seemed as if the intention was to slap your face. One of the new ways of greeting someone in Europe is to flash them a quick smile, over in a second, and then one's face goes back to normal. This is often so artificial that it seems they smile only because they know it teases. But everyone had got used to this: the quick meaningless smile and the instant return to solemnity. If you met Louis's mother, this was how she would greet you. Louis, too, would flash his teeth and go grave again and look at his mother. At first, I didn't get it but later I understood. His mother had a pleasant face and a sweet smile when it was real. But this rictus of politeness made her look ugly. When

Louis reshaped his face into a similar grotesque shape, he offered a critique—could he be wholly unconscious of it?—of this greeting.

That evening there was a tea-dance. Louis's mother danced her heart out with Mandal. It seemed as if the Jews were intent on savouring every happy moment, trying to extract every last joy out of the present. At the end, while saying her farewells, she offered her heartfelt thanks to Mandal. He was touched and raised her hands to his lips. She was carrying Louis in her arms. Mandal wished the little boy a good night too and put out his hand. The little fellow took the proffered hand in the right style and then bit it severely. Whether he thought he was simply doing what was ordinarily done when you brought someone's hand to your mouth or whether he was warning Mandal off was not clear. But Shinde, who was also around, laughed uproariously. He went up and took Louis in a bear hug and said to me, 'You see? Jewish children don't like strange men making passes at their mothers.'

I laughed and replied, 'Perhaps. But what has that to do with me?'

'You're being watched. That's all I can say.'

'I'm watching you too,' I said.

'Meaning?'

'You remember that line: "Good boy, better mummy"? You praise Louis, you get to his mother.'

'Don't worry about that,' Shinde said with a laugh. 'Louis is a good watchdog. If I cross any lines, he'll bite me, good and hard. Right, Louis?'

Louis nodded. In the middle of his forehead, a curl bobbed like a spring. He said, 'Ja.'

Shinde tickled him and said, 'I swear I'm going to get this little fellow to say at least one English word. Come on, Louis, say, "Yes".'

But Louis caught on. Resisting this new language came easily to him. Shinde pinched his cheek affectionately and said, 'Just you wait, my fine fellow. I'm going to get some English out of you today.'

He took Louis off to the piano and seating

the boy on his knee, he began to play. I went to stand next to them should I be needed for *Chopsticks*. The music drew some couples to us. They began to dance. Shinde stepped up the tempo. The rhythm got faster. Louis started to clap to the rhythm. I picked him up and took him on my hip. With one of his small hands in mine, I joined the dance.

It was now going with a swing. Shinde also got caught up in the spirit of things. Louis let go, shrieking with joy, as if he were echoing the collective release everyone felt in this impromptu dance.

Then the piano stopped. I put Louis down and he ran off to Shinde again and commanded him to start.

'Should I play, Louis?' Shinde asked.

'Ja, ja.'

Shinde plinked a single note.

'Only if you say, "Yes". So, Louis, should I play?'

'Yes,' Louis said immediately.

Shinde plinked and plonked and plinked again.

'More?'

'Ja,' said Louis and then seeing the music begin to slip away: 'Yes.'

'Say "Uncle, play the piano"', said Shinde.

Now Louis was willing to pay the price for his desires.

'Uncle, play the piano.'

Victory to Shinde! All of Louis' objections to English seem to have evaporated.

'Now say, "I like the piano".'

'I like the piano.'

'I like English.'

'I like English.'

'Very much.'

'Very much.'

Shinde took pity on Louis. He drew the boy to him and hugged him, 'Ah, you're a sweet chap.'

Louis didn't get it. He said: 'Ah, you're a sweet chap.'

Everyone began to laugh. Shinde picked him up and said to me, 'By the morning, he'll be an English professor.'

'Morning? Aren't you getting off at Port Said?'

'Of course. But let's take him along. What say, Louis? Say yes.'

A touch on my shoulder. Herta.

Her appearance surprised me. Her hair was combed. She had a floral ribbon arranged artfully as a tiara across her dark hair. She had changed her clothes and was now wearing a thin silk shift that flowed to her ankles. It was sleeveless, backless and low-necked. She had a black fur wrapped around her shoulders and even a corsage.

Mannan was with her. He was still wearing the suit he had had on at dinner. They looked ready for the ball. Herta preened a little.

'I wanted to ask you something,' she said. 'Guess what it is.'

Mannan raised his eyebrows. It was clear that he did not like this. I said deliberately, 'If you're going to ask me to dance, I will have to disappoint you. I don't know how.'

She led me over to a table and sat me down.

Mannan followed. She said, 'It wasn't that. I'm asking everyone. I even asked Mr Mannan here. Now it's your turn. How do I look?'

'As if you've found your luggage,' I said.

She turned solemn again. Mannan said, 'That was rather rude.'

I got up. 'I'm sorry,' I said, addressing them both. 'I meant no rudeness. I knew your luggage had been lost and was happy for you that it seemed to have been restored to you. That's all.'

So saying, I bade them goodnight and left the bar to stand on the deck. Port Said was approaching. The sea was growing young again, burrowing into the land as a baby nuzzles into its mother.

Herta came to stand next to me. 'I want to tell you something, Bob.'

'Go on.'

'Wait, I just want to be sure no one is listening,' she looked all around. Then she took my hand and said in a small solemn voice. 'I'm going to tell you but you must promise never to tell anyone else.'

'I'll try.'

'Bob, don't tell anyone but I really do not like you.'

'I won't tell anyone but I do wish you would tell just one person.'

'Who?'

'Mannan.'

She took hold of my shoulders and kissed me gently. 'I'm so relieved. You must have been jealous, no? I find I like to torment you a little. I waited for you on the deck but you didn't turn up, did you?'

I moved away a little and said, 'Wrong. I did come up and I did look for you. You were nowhere on the deck.'

'After dinner, I stood for two hours by that pillar over there.'

'Did you? Perhaps you did. But how was I to see you? You should have equipped yourself with a lamp as any self-respecting lighthouse would.'

She moved away and looked out over the sea. Then she said, 'Do you need to see a face to tell it is someone who is your own? When you love, everything, the shape of the body, how it moves, all of it comes alive in the mind. Is there any dearth of darkness here, for instance? And yet, I found you unerringly. I have the feeling that you don't really care for me.'

'No, I really don't,' I said, putting out my pipe, tucking it away and drawing her close.

In a while she said, 'I asked Mr Mannan how I looked. He said, "Very beautiful." You still haven't told me how I look.'

I said casually, 'Lady, you don't look any different. You look like any other human being.'

Her face turned intense. She grabbed me and said: 'Bob, you're a mind-reader. That's just what I was thinking. I have become human again. Over the last four or five years, I had grown used to being treated as the lowest of the low, the unwanted, the outcaste. And then I set foot on the ship. I began to inhale the fresh air of freedom. I couldn't believe it. Everyone here acknowledges me, talks to me, laughs with me, plays with me. You adore me, you take care of me. You care what happens to me. Look, I'm a human being again.'

I was startled. Her intensity grew. She rested her head on my shoulder and began to speak again. 'They found my luggage today. And my clothes. Let's get down at Port Said. I have what it takes to be happy. And I'm ready for some happiness. Let's get back on terra firma. Let's roam, run, play, dance...everything. I know all the things I've longed to do. Let's sip coffee in a café and talk philosophy. Let's watch a play in a theatre. Let's go to a nightclub and dance. And...and what else? Yes, during a peaceful stretch of the night, let's find an empty street and run wild. Or a beach. That's it. We'll find a beach and I shall stand by your side. No, like a statue of de Lesseps, I shall stand in front of the ship and say, "Bob, this is the Suez, the door to the East. Germany is behind us. Europe is a memory. I have left behind a culture that belittled me, humiliated me and which lives by 'Might is right'. I am now in another continent for 'Eastward look the land is bright"'.

I held her tight. The ship had stopped. A flotilla of small boats swarmed up to the ship.

Egyptian hawkers were yowling about the merits of their wares. We got ready to descend. I told Herta, 'Mannan might disapprove. Go with him in the launch and I will meet you ashore.'

~

Port Said did not have a jetty. Ships stood out at sea and motor launches ferried passengers to land. Everyone was ready, including Keitel. I asked, 'You were not going to come?'

'I made some inquiries,' Keitel said with a laugh. 'The launch is free. So the matter was resolved.'

All the Germans were in a hurry. They were eager to get off. Shinde had Louis on his hip. The boy was wearing a thin navy-blue outfit. His mother was standing with the Jews. So were Herta and Mannan.

The ship was terribly hot below deck but when I came up, a cold wind was blowing. I said to Louis's mother, 'We'll be late. It's getting chilly. Take something to keep Louis warm. If we move quickly, we'll get place in the first launch.'

The first-class passengers were crowding the upper deck. Uniformed officials, customs officers in Turkish fezzes, immigration officers, all the passengers in wonderful clothes, all eager to get on to land.

Ladders had been set up to help us descend into the launches. We were all in line. It was our turn. Shinde was behind me. I showed my passport and was given a card of permission. Shinde likewise. The officer asked about Louis. Shinde said, 'His mother is in the line behind us. We're catching a seat on the launch.'

After some debate, Shinde was allowed to climb down the rope ladder. Planks had been lashed together to form a pontoon stand and the launches had been drawn up to it. Since his arms were tiring, Shinde wasted no time getting into the launch. Louis was in seventh heaven. Shinde found a corner seat and put him down. Other passengers followed but not Louis's mother. The launch was soon full. Shinde looked at me, worried. There was no way to return. I shouted, 'Don't worry. Go on. I'll find her and follow.'

The launch left. The second launch arrived. I could not make my way up. There were crowds everywhere, on the ladders, on the deck. Next to me was an Englishman in a dinner suit, his eyes red from drinking. He seemed unsteady on his feet. Then he collapsed. I grabbed him to steady him and laid him down. He started to convulse. Everyone began to shout for a doctor. I loosened his tie and freed his neck of its constricting collar. I splashed his face with water. Launches came and went but I paid no heed. Only when the Englishman regained some bleary semblance of consciousness did I look up. A launch had just left. The crowds had evaporated. An Egyptian sepoy was at the top of the ladder with an officer in white uniform next to him.

The ladders were empty. I asked a sailor, 'When will the next launch come?'

'In half an hour.'

I went up on deck and the steward asked, 'Didn't go?'

I shook my head and went in. Just then a female voice said, 'Hello.'

It was Louis's mother

'Well done,' I said. 'It's very late now but let's go.'

She kept looking at me.

'What is it? Why aren't you speaking? It's gone cold. You'll need something to keep Louis warm. Get it and let's go.'

'Go where?'

'Port Said, of course.'

'Not allowed,' she said in a tearful voice.

'Who says so?'

'Everyone.'

I was shocked.

'You have a passport, right? Come on then. Who's to stop you?'

I took her hand and we went to the ladder. The usual officer, the usual interrogation.

'Passport?'

I proffered mine. He looked at the gold inscription on the cover and said, 'British? Go right ahead, sir.'

He looked at her and said, 'British passport, madam?'

She was so frightened her hands were trembling.

'I think it's German,' I said.

He raised an eyebrow. He opened her passport, took a look and returned it saying, 'I thought so. I'm sorry I cannot let you set foot on these shores.'

I was stumped. Louis's mother could not even take her passport back, she was so shaken. She kept looking at both of us as if she did not understand. Finally, one of the officers touched her on the elbow and said, 'Please, madam,' and moved her out of the way.

I tried to argue with the official. I pointed out that her son was already on shore but his answer was unvarying. 'I'm sorry, sir, but German Jews are not allowed on these shores.' I offered to take responsibility for bringing her back again. 'My orders are strict. I'm sorry.' I stood on the deck by the rails. I could not even speak to her. My mind was full of anger and frustration. I took out my pipe. On the other side of the deck, a small crowd of white people had gathered around an Arab in a fez who was laughing. Some bits of their conversation drifted over to where I was standing.

'But what is our sin? You won't even let us go ashore?'

'Who will guarantee that you will return?' asked the Arab.

'Where do you think we'll go?'

'Who knows? You lot are refugees. You could sneak off anywhere. You'll take shelter where you find it. What if you enter Palestine?'

They were silent and then someone said angrily: 'We are no outsiders to Palestine. Historically, it was the home of the Jews.'

The Arab laughed sarcastically and shrugged. 'Really? That must have been before my time. All I know is that today Palestine belongs to the Arabs.'

Who knows who had the right of it? Before the Romans came, before the Muslims, history attests to the fact that Palestine was a Jewish country. But history has many faces. No nation can give evidence of ownership.

~

But where was Herta? On her face were the marks of her sufferings. She had left Germany and once more begun to experience the joys of freedom. And here again, a shock. I began to worry that she would lose courage and all the suppressed rage might explode into some form of madness. I went looking for her and found everyone else, all their faces woeful as if they had been expecting this unpleasantness.

Louis's mother was worried about her son. Hermann was making fun of his wife. 'Look how she's dressed up,' he said. 'Who was going to look at her in the middle of the night in Port Said?'

She frowned and said, 'I wanted to post a letter.'

He said, 'There are post-boxes on board the ship.'

Keitel saw me and smiled wryly. He said: 'I'm just annoyed because I didn't get my beauty sleep.'

Finally, I spotted Herta on deck. I called to her from a distance. She made no response. I went up and touched her arm. She turned, unseeing for a moment and then reached out as if to assure herself that it were really me. Then she came to her senses and said, 'Bob!'

She turned away again. Her lips were pressed together. Her arms formed a swastika across her chest as if she were holding herself together. In a while she said, 'Why did you come into my life? If someone pays attention to you, you become aware that you are human. Then they kick you in the knees again.'

I freed myself from her grasp and took her hand in mine.

'What can I say, Herta?'

There was very little light. I could see drops of blood on her hand.

'What's this, love?' I asked.

She looked at her hand and said: 'I must have bitten myself.'

I looked at them angrily, helplessly, these marks of a rage turned in on itself, and said, 'Herta, have you gone mad?'

She took out her handkerchief and wiped the blood away. Then she said, 'I have a request,

Bob. Let's just not talk about what happened ever again.'

She had told me many things about her life in Germany. But her demons had not been exorcised. Perhaps she felt that displaying her sorrow would be tantamount to admitting her helplessness. But just as you remove a thorn embedded in your flesh with hot oil, my affection drew out her sorrow. We stood on the deck, each lost in thought until she said, 'A penny for them?'

I said, 'Have you ever seen Hitler? Do you like him?'

She was startled but she could see that it was not my intention to hurt her. She could sense my confusion. 'Oh, I love Hitler,' she said. 'If I met him, I would kiss him.'

Her voice was savage with a welter of emotions: her suppressed rage, the desire for revenge, the inability to take it, the personal helplessness of an individual against Nazi-sponsored hate. I felt that if it came to that, Herta would have no hesitation in becoming a vishkanya and were she really to meet Hitler, she might inflict upon him the kiss of death.

There was a ring on her finger, I saw now. Not gold, certainly, not platinum either. I did not think she would wear just any old ring either. I lifted her hand and looked at it.

'What are you looking at?' she asked.

'I was going to ask,' I said. 'But it's bad form to ask personal questions.'

'Oh yes, our relationship is circumscribed by these conventions,' she said.

'I was going to ask about your ring.'

She freed her hand and raised it to look at the ring. She seemed a little disturbed. 'You haven't asked but I will tell you anyway. Someone gave it to me.'

'I'm not that eager to know who.'

'Thanks,' she said and smiled. 'You're a true gentleman. But I might even feel better for telling you.'

'Go on then,' I said and took her hand in mine again.

~

She took off the ring and held it up for my inspection.

'See the letters? K and F? For Karl Franz. You won't get angry, Bob? There's no need. You are my love now but when I left Germany, he was. Women don't do things by half-measures, I think, and I was madly in love with him. I accepted Karl and we made promises to each other. This ring is a sign of those promises. When he gave it to me, it was platinum. But we were not allowed to take any valuables out of the country. When I was exiled, my money, my jewellery, even that ring, all of it was taken from me. As a mark of that theft, I got this, an ordinary ring made of base metal. That's what I wear.'

Without knowing it, I had moved away. I had told myself I did not love her so why had I moved away on hearing of Franz? She must have felt the same for she did not try to approach me. She said, 'You said you would listen. I have no one to talk to freely. And yet my mind is alive. It thirsts for companionship. How much must I starve it? How much must I bear? These new experiences are like shocks to the mind. Sometimes I wonder whether we have any control over our circumstances. Franz was everything to me at one point. I still remember him. But today I am totally yours. Does that mean anything?'

Once again, Uma's letter arose in my mind. After so many years, in another time, in another woman's voice, the same words.

I saw that she was leaning on the rail, looking down at the water. I took her in my arms again. After a while, we went to sit on a pile of rope. I gave her a cigarette and lit my pipe. Her heart was full and she began to talk.

# Four

In my words then, her story:

August now. Everywhere the fields and meadows have absorbed the heat and the scythes begin to fall on the standing grain. Once the season ends, the war will begin, or so everyone says. Germany is rearming. Death bides its time, eager for a bloody harvest.

It was time for the Milan Express to leave. The station was quiet. A few passengers turned up and got into their carriages silently. There were no crowds on the platforms, no hawkers' cries. The railway officials, the policemen and the plain-clothes secret police were present as always. A bunch of pleasure seekers on their way to a holiday in Italy and Switzerland were getting into the train. All of them were going only to return to Germany at some point. But fifteen to twenty passengers will not be allowed to return. They were German Jews who were being deported. One of them was Herta's seventy-five-year-old mother, walking with difficulty. Herta urged her gently into the train compartment, kissing her and murmuring, 'Mutti, Mutti' to encourage her onwards.

The compartment was not very full. Herta spied a suitable spot in the third-class carriage. As her mother was about to sit down, she glanced at the cushions and said, 'These are not for us.' Herta sat her down anyway and said she was going to see about the luggage. It wasn't actually the luggage she was looking for. She was looking for Franz. For a German Christian to even come to the station to see a Jew off would be asking for trouble. But hope still rose in Herta's breast. Just then a porter put a note into her hand and said quietly, 'From Herr Franz.' She slipped the note into her blouse and looked around. To avoid suspicion she turned to the train again. At the door an official, his voice expressionless, his face stern, stopped her. 'Fraulein?'

'Yes?'

'We have to check your entire luggage. You will get your bags back at Naples.'

'But I have nothing to wear. Only the clothes on my body. Even my mother's medicines are in our luggage.'

'That can't be helped. You will get your luggage in Naples, the day after tomorrow.'

He was staring at her. She did not have the courage to meet his eyes.

'And Fraulein?' he said, 'Tonight when we cross the German border, there will be another check. Money, gold, jewellery, you can take none of these abroad with you. It would be best to declare anything now.'

He waited for a reply. She said nothing. He turned away. Just then a man in plain clothes arrived. He snapped off a Nazi salute and said, 'That note you received five minutes ago? Hand it over, please.'

Unwittingly, Herta's hand leapt to her breast. She could say nothing. Her eyes darted about.

The official said, 'We have no desire to harass you. But it would be best to hand over that note.'

She could say nothing. He went on. 'If you do not hand it over of your own free will, we will have to arrest you. Your old mother will have to travel to Shanghai on her own, if she lives that long.'

She took out the letter and gave it to him. As she did so, she said, 'At least let me read it once.'

The officers left without another word.

Five minutes now to departure. Some Indian students raced up and jumped into the train. They had a quantity of luggage with them. For a while, Herta kept looking at the luggage trolley with envy. As it emptied, she was startled. On the other side, at a small bookstall, Karl was standing, pretending to browse but his eyes were seeking her.

Herta hastened towards him but he turned his face away. She stopped. Recognizing him might be dangerous. She thought for a while and then went forward anyway.

'Karl,' she called.

He looked at her startled.

Speaking with difficulty now, she continued,

'Karl, there's no help for it. Your letter is in the hands of the Gestapo.'

His face blanched. He could say nothing. They stood there looking at each other, their last precious moments together lost in madness. The train began to move. Without even saying goodbye, Herta had to jump in.

~

In dreams, one sees everything except for one's own face. Memories operate in the same way. Herta remembered everything but she could no longer conjure up Karl's face. She could remember his deep blue eyes, his close-cropped hair. She remembered the army uniform he used to wear. But whatever she did, she could not bring his face into focus. The train began to race but Herta was still standing where she was. What had been in the letter?

What if he had written something incriminating? Ever since the declaration forbidding German Christians to have any relations with Jews, Franz had been forced to avoid her. The declaration had killed their one-and-a-half-year-old love. Would Karl suffer for his letter? What if he had written something like, 'I will never let you go, come what may. I can forsake Germany but I could never forsake you'? What then? Jail? Or...

Her skin crawled at the possibilities. Such stories came to one's ears. The Gestapo stopped at nothing. The fear was so real that she felt she might actually scream. Her hands sprang to her face to muffle it. Her fingers were cold but even colder was the ring on her finger that touched her lips. The officer who had given her the replacement ring had said with a sneer, 'Fraulein, Germany needs every ounce of metal today for arms. At least this is metal of some kind. The German government is willing to make this sacrifice for you.'

Karl had been her first love. A delicate love that should have perhaps remained hidden. Perhaps she herself had cast an evil eye on it. She had met him first when she had gone for a tramp in the Salzburg Woods. Darkness had begun to fall. Winter days. The air was thick with woodland fragrances. Both of them had lost their way. They were tired and seemed to be getting further and further lost. Finally, at the bank of a stream, they took out their snacks. Herta peeled a banana and threw the peel away casually.

Karl said, 'I love my country and I don't like you dirtying it up like that.'

She replied simply, 'My father gave his life fighting for Germany in the last World War.'

Karl took her hand and said, 'I'm sorry. I knew you were Jewish but now I know you're a German.'

After their snacks were eaten they set out again.

They began to sing the new songs of victory to the Reich. Somewhere along that walk, he took her hand. They found their steps matched each other's. Night fell and made finding their bearings even more difficult. Something slithered through the undergrowth. Terrified, she clung to Franz. He held her close and kissed her. Her eyes had begun to fill with tears but the shelter of his embrace slowly calmed her as if it were a suit of impregnable armour. The light touch of his lips drove the fear out of her. In those moments she felt liberated.

Herta believed that a woman's love is born once and then it dies. Her dedication is complete and without inflection. Herta had found an excitement flowing through her when she discovered herself to be in love with Franz. She felt as if the world was suddenly her oyster.

~

Then the Milan Express whistled and the high-pitched shriek dragged her back to her new reality. It had begun to grow dark. A railway official went from carriage to carriage announcing dinner, 'First service.' He came to the last compartment. The toilet attendant said, 'Why go further? There are only Jews there. They'd starve rather than spend.'

Keitel was standing in the passage. He had heard what the toilet attendant had said. He turned and went back to his seat. He was about fifty years old, tall, balding with a true German beer belly. He had had a good life in Germany until the Jews had begun to be exterminated.

He had lost his job. His savings had been seized by the government. With half his life behind him, he was being forced to reinvent himself.

He was easy-going by nature, adaptable, willing to change as circumstances demanded. He had already begun to plan his future life. He went to the compartment and opened the door. There were only two people there.

Frau and Herr Hermann were sitting in a close embrace. He was feeding her a loaf of bread. They did not move apart even when Keitel entered. In the past two years, the Jews of Germany had lost the habit of privacy. Everywhere they went they were greeted with suspicious looks and stares of dislike. Even a married couple would find it difficult to find moments in which to be intimate. How could they? They had lost their homes. Hotels and restaurants and theatres were closed to them. Only the gardens and the streets remained and even there, they faced restrictions.

Keitel returned to the corridor. In the next compartment, Herta's mother was alone. Her head was covered with scanty white hair, the colour of the ash of the emotions of a lifetime. She had no great regrets about leaving Berlin; how did it matter, she seemed to suggest by her very demeanour, where one's grave is dug. Her eyes were rheumy, distant, as if lacking even the will to sleep. Her lips drooped, leather slashed by uncaring scissors. When Keitel entered she looked up, hoping to see Herta. When she saw a stranger, she looked away disappointed.

Keitel sat down and looked at the old lady who was shivering. The air had turned cold. He got up and closed the door and shut the window. Above them was a copper handle attached to a vent that released a current of warm air. He reached up to turn that on when she spoke, 'No, don't. Perhaps we are not allowed. Perhaps warm air is only for the Nazis.'

He sat down again and asked if she had eaten.

She had not, so he returned to his compartment and brought his snacks. There wasn't much: some bread, a couple of eggs and sandwiches. The old lady took whatever she was offered and both of them ate as much as they could. From time to time, they spoke but it was always bad news. Neither was surprised by the news of further curbs on the movements of Jews. Just last week it had been announced that the public toilets and urinals were closed to Jews. This further restricted the movement of women.

~

It was around 11 p.m. Over the thump and thud of the train, Marthe could hear the sound of groaning from the compartment in which Herta and her mother were. She woke her mother up and sent her to find out. As her mother left, Marthe told her to see if she could find Keitel.

Keitel returned and then Marthe's mother came back, shuddering as if she had witnessed something filthy. As soon as she saw Keitel she said, 'Don't trust these brats. Where that Herta is, I just don't know. And there her mother is suffering all alone.'

A little earlier, Herta's mother had woken up with a pain in her stomach. Her stomach began to hurt. Her chest felt compressed too. She was alone in the compartment. It was difficult for her to get up and go out but there was no help for it. She opened the door and stepped into the corridor. The toilet and bathroom were at the end of the carriage. It was dark now but she could still see the uniform of a railway official. Frightened, she returned to the compartment. Her stomach began to cramp and she moaned in pain. This was what Marthe had heard in the next compartment.

Now Marthe began to laugh. Keitel said angrily, 'What are you laughing about? Those gold teeth may be taken from you if you flash them about. That'll teach you.'

When Herta returned, her mother's suffering shook her. This was only the first day of their exile. They had not even left Germany's borders. And the rest of her life was to be spent in an unknown, as-yet-undecided land. What if they made this their last day? Suicide was an ever-present possibility but it is never as easy as it sounds. Had it been, she would have taken that way out. Twice, she had found herself at that dark threshold. The last time had been only a few days ago.

~

Their house was burning.

They lived in a Jewish neighbourhood in a suburban by-lane. Outside, she saw that it wasn't just her home that was on fire. The entire neighbourhood was filled with Jewish homes. Two or three others were burning too. This was not unexpected. Stones were thrown, windows collapsed in heaps of glass, doors stripped. It was terrifying even to open the door to go out. One did not know what one might see outside. But returning home was also difficult. What might have happened while one had been away?

Herta had been alone in the house when her house had been set alight. She escaped by the backdoor. Her mother had been visiting friends. She could hardly see anything but she took shelter under a tree. People gathered in the dark. Some were scared. Some were simply watching. Some were giggling nervously. But none of them tried to put out the fires. The fire brigade must have been informed but no help came. To help the Jews was to invite trouble.

The houses burned brightly. They were soon reduced to ash. In front of their eyes. Their homes had been labelled: Jew house. Over that someone would write later: Jews once lived here.

Herta's heart was aflame with rage. Why should I burn in this fire? she asked herself. The burning of the houses was the climax. At first, she had heard about all this, stories of public insults and private humiliations. Then it began to happen to her. People began to point and stare. Jews lost their jobs. They could not find homes to rent. Restaurants closed their doors. Theatres carried large signs: Jews not allowed.

A little later, she lost her job. Her employer was a gentleman. As Herr Nober bade her farewell, he said, 'Come to me the day you have to leave Germany. I would give you money but you will not be allowed to take it out of the country. I could give you a testimonial but I will have to ask you not to show it to anyone in Germany or I might get into trouble.'

Without a job, the days grew long and bleak. Franz was her only support. It gave her courage just to meet him and talk to him.

'Herta, don't worry. It's just a phase. This madness will pass. Everything will go back to normal,' he would say.

And it was on that day that the law forbidding Aryans to have any relations with Jews was passed. His words rang hollow now. Her last support had been withdrawn. She wanted to weep, to scream her rage, but where? As long as they had had a home, she could retreat to it to cry but then they lost their home too and there was nowhere to weep. She was helpless, she did not know where to go.

The night the law was passed, Herta found herself on the streets. They were quiet.

Preparations for war were on and so they were lit with twinkling blue lights. Rows and rows of twinkling blue lights.

Herta began to walk. She did not know how long she walked. She walked until she was exhausted, her fatigue compounding her misery and loneliness. Just the act of thinking numbed her. The quietness had an ominous quality to it. Winter had descended. The shadows of the trees were long on the street. The dust had been tamped down by the moisture in the air. What was left of it, refracted the light. The dust was like a carpet. The stones gleamed white. She was walking on a carpet, she was surrounded by carpets.

This was the beginning of madness, she realized, and gave herself a mental shake.

'What nonsense,' she said to herself. 'The road is beautiful but it is not a carpet. The beauty is real, the carpet is false.'

What is truth and what is falsehood? Herta felt she was experiencing a state in which both could apply to the same thing. From time to time, a car would pass and the reflection of its headlamps would fall on the asphalt road, rays that were clear, clean, sharp as knives. The knives were meant for her. And yet as soon as the car passed, it would look like a toy, a beautiful toy. The trees were ghostly sentinels. The windows of the houses were lit but as she passed they seemed to go out.

'They are going out because I pass,' she said to herself. And inside, another voice replied: 'Are you mad? They're just going to sleep.' But she could not quell the feeling that the lights went out because of her.

She had eaten nothing. 'No relationships with Aryans?' she thought, 'But Franz is an Aryan. He's getting threatening letters. His life is in danger because of me.'

The thought pursued her relentlessly.

'Have I lost him?' she wondered desperately. 'His embrace? His protection? Must I lose the only truthful thing in my life? Must I lose my only place of refuge? Then what is left for me?'

The houses looked like pictures, the streets

ribbons of darkness. In the blue light one could make out the creepers in the gardens, shining with dew. They seemed ready to take flight. Sometimes the sound of footsteps would ring in her ears and make her turn around. Who knew who might be there? But no one spoke to her; no one even noticed her existence. Sometimes she would wonder, 'Have I evaporated? Am I walking around without a body?'

'Nonsense,' another part of her would reply, 'this is Berlin. How can it be that no one is looking at you?'

But when she met some disreputable young women, she would envy the attention they attracted. She wished someone would ask her to come with him.

'I might refuse,' she told herself. 'But even saying "No" would mean hearing my own voice.'

But no one looked at her. In front of her now, a garden, ablaze with flowers, brilliant even in the blue half-light. She stopped to stand and stare, an old habit. The law forbidding Jews to sit on park benches was now an old one. But still there rose in her the urge to sit on a park bench.

'If I am alive,' she said to herself, 'surely someone will notice me, someone will drive me away.'

She sat down and waited but no one noticed, no one asked her to move. What could this mean? A cold breeze was blowing but her delusion persisted.

'No room for me,' she thought. 'No eating here. No looking at that. No living here. Am I allowed the breeze? How can it be blowing on me? Does it not know that I am a Jew?'

She got up again and began to walk. The cars skimmed by her but she was not afraid of them. They were not of her world. She could not tell whether the passers-by were men or women. They were not of her time. Her world was different.

'How can it be that not one person looks at me in the whole of Berlin? These are the same streets I have walked so often. We lost the last War. On these very streets, we wept as a nation, hugging each other, holding strangers, consoling ourselves, consoling them. I remember that War. I remember when my father enlisted. I was still a toddler. People who knew us showed their respect and Mother held her head high. I would tell my friends that my father was away, fighting for his motherland. Then he was killed. We were on the bus. Mother had a friend, a German woman. She saw Mother and gave her a hug. She kissed both her cheeks and said, "*Mutti*, *Mutti*" in consolation. Was that true? Is this?

'The same fingers. The same eyes. My poor mother, seventy-five years now. She's kneeling in the street trying to clear away the snow. Snow is falling. Deep winter. So much snow.

'No,' she said sternly. 'These images are false. If it were deep winter and my poor mother were out in the street, she might have died. Or at least suffered a terrible attack of rheumatism.'

Stones flew at windowpanes, small explosions of glass and cold air. From the window, dirt fell on her bed.

'Were these images false? The world is false.

The world's categories are false. We are not Jews. We are Germans.

'What of that old world? So many years spent in it. Was that not life? But when I look at myself, why does this hurt? Sometimes, I slam my body against the walls just to feel pain. Is this pain true or false? Little truths add up to the grand illusion. Home gone. Karl gone. Citizenship gone. This duality is tiring. The moth suffers so much. Why can I not destroy this false world? I can. It would not be suicide. Murder, suicide...such big words. Kill a man and it is called murder. Squash an insect and who notices?'

A tube station appeared. Those dark tunnels would be a good place to put an end to it all. She went in. In the anonymous and forgiving dark, no one would know.

It was close to dawn. She went to the bathroom. In a huge mirror there, she looked at herself. She could not believe what she saw. This body, all five-and-a-half feet of it, all hers. What a republic of one. What a gift it was! Her body, her head, her feet, all grew large and began to fill her eyes. Destroy it all? What a task that would be! Such madness!

For a long time, she looked at herself. Finally she wet her head under the tap and felt sense flooding back. She had been saved only because she had lost her way.

# Five

I came on deck after breakfast. On the way, I met Mannan. He was saying something to Herta. First she pretended not to hear but he persisted and finally, she said, 'I must thank you. But I have no wish to do that. I have not the habit of begging.'

Keitel was laughing. I asked him why. He said, 'Sufferance may be the badge of all our tribe but we will not suffer anyone's charity.'

A committee of Jews, residents of Port Said, had been constituted to help the refugees. In the middle of the night, they had sent bundles of clothes and some money, along with messages of support. All the Jews came on deck. One of them read out the message. They opened the bundles: most were old clothes. The monetary aid amounted to twenty-five rupees. Each person got about a rupee and twelve annas.

The division of the spoils began. The women were in the thick of it, looking at the clothes, testing them. Squabbles broke out and compromises were reached. Every one of them had been earning until a couple of years ago but within a short time, they had been reduced to the mentality of beggars. Only two people stayed out of it: Herta and her mother.

The ship was passing through the Suez Canal. There was a change in the air. On either side, there were groves of date palms. On the right, the Suez Railway. Small stations would appear, trees clustered around them. That was about all the greenery to be seen. Otherwise the lone and level sands stretched far away. The heat increased. A hot breeze began to blow. The passengers, fresh out of Europe, began to feel the effects of it. By afternoon, they were all in a state of collapse, lying around the deck as if felled.

That evening, three or four Indians were standing around talking about helping the Jews.

Sahai said mischievously, 'I think Chakradhar and Madnani should be excused from any collection we make.'

Michael put on his best innocent look and asked, 'Why? If we collect, we should all contribute.'

Chatterjee took up the baton of badinage. 'Let's leave them out. They're trying to do what they can in their individual capacity.'

Jadhav said, 'Stop it. Let me make a list. Mandal, you first. How much should I put you down for?'

Yogeshwar Mandal was standing by the railing, looking out to sea. 'I have no wish to help traitors,' he said, sharply.

Everyone was startled. Sahai had taken out his fountain pen and he now recapped it and said ironically: 'You were in Germany for only two years. Was that all the time it took to turn you into a Nazi?'

Mandal replied, 'You don't have to be a Nazi to hate traitors.'

Michael shook his head, dismissing Mandal

as beyond all help. Chatterjee laughed and said, 'You seem to have studied *Mein Kampf* rather well.'

'It isn't as if only Hitler says that the Jews destroyed Germany. All the Germans say it.'

'And how do they say that the Jews managed to do that?'

'What didn't they do?' Mandal demanded. 'In the last War, it was the Jews who slit Germany's throat. They sold German war secrets to the enemies. They forced war debt on to the world to keep the War going and grew rich on the interest. It was in Jewish factories that the bombs that rained down on Germany were made. The uniforms they supplied the German army? The boots they made? Stuffed with the bark of trees. They supplied third-rate food grain, unfit for human consumption, to the army. Even the tobacco was sawdust. That their greed was hollowing Germany out meant nothing to them.'

Shinde said quietly: 'All this can't be attributed to the Jews alone. The greed for profit is at the basis of all society. Why do you assume that this happened only in the case of Germany? The same things happened in England too. At the time of War, American companies were given many contracts to supply war ordnance. Many of those companies had German capital invested in them. You just spread a rumour that will help you secure the contract. What you said about the food grain? That would have happened in England too. And their uniforms and shoes would have been just as bad.'

Michael joined the fray: 'Why talk about England and France and Germany? What happened in Hindustan? When the Non-Cooperation Movement was on, weren't people's sentiments exploited? Mill cloth was sold as khadi, Japanese cloth was labelled as swadeshi. Wasn't that dirty business too? Are you going to exterminate all these people?'

Mandal was silent but his eyes were red. In a firm voice, he said, 'We certainly will. We will remember all those who put their personal agendas before the national interest. And we will take revenge.'

Michael asked irritably: 'And how many Hindustanis have you met who put nation before self?'

Mandal's tone was equally irritable: 'I know that. I can tell you who sacrifices the good of the nation for selfish motives.'

Mannan sought to add fuel to the flames. 'Speak out then if you have the courage.'

'What need for courage? There are enough greedy people among us who claim greater rights because of their minority status. They don't mind if it means that independence is delayed just so long as they get what they want. That's the sum of their national philosophy.'

Mannan interrupted vehemently: 'So you're suggesting they should be treated as the Jews are treated in Nazi Germany?'

'They should know that if they don't come to their senses, they will meet with the same fate, make no mistake,' said Mandal.

Michael could not take Mandal's jibes about minorities lightly. 'Do you know where that will end?' he asked.

'I'll tell you,' said Mannan. 'Palestine once belonged to the Jews. Today it belongs to the Arabs. Hindustan also could end up with a different name. Today the Congress is tormenting the Parsis, the Christians and Muslims so much, it might happen in the next generation.'

Shinde was red with rage. He said to Mannan: 'Perhaps that name might even be changed. But make no mistake, those who seek to change its name for another, will also die.'

We were standing at the railing. Another ship came alongside us. It was very close. There were sailors on the decks of both ships. Since it was near lunchtime, there were knives and forks in the hands of many of the sailors. Now that we were within earshot, on both ships, the shouting began. Threats were exchanged. From the gestures, it seemed apparent that necks and sundry other parts were to be slashed.

It was a French ship; ours was Italian. Someone on board our ship called out a remark derogatory to France. Two French sailors climbed on to the rail. One of them began to imitate Mussolini's speech-making style. The other pretended to lick his mate's boots while striking himself on the chest and mumbling, '*Il Duce, Il Duce*'. The ersatz Mussolini opened his jaws so wide, he seemed unable to shut them again. His mate climbed on to the rail and boxed him under his chin to help him close his mouth. 'Idiot,' he said, 'Why open your mouth so wide?' Suddenly the sailors were galvanized into action and began to hurl whatever they could find at each other. When we got to the scene of battle, it had reached its peak. It was only the discipline of the sea that saved us that day. Slowly the other ship dropped behind us.

The idea of helping the Jews was stillborn. It seemed as if this were a European war and we could not be bothered about it. I didn't think so. If Europe were ablaze, Hindustan would burn too. If the Jews were in trouble, so would we be. It was with this disquieting thought that I fell asleep, only to dream I was sitting at the mouth of Mt Vesuvius and dreaming while beneath me, lava swelled and roiled.

~

In the morning, Louis's mother came to my cabin. 'The doctor wants you,' she said.

The cold air of Port Said had left Louis ill. Dr Shinde had spent the night by his bed. But it was a woman's cabin and therein lay the rub.

Louis was brought to my cabin. His mother, Dr Shinde and I treated him, sharing shifts. His mother was on duty for all twenty-four hours. I tried to get her to take a break but to no avail. We spent that day with a fretful child.

The next day, his fever still raged on. He did not smile now and his face was wan and pale. The heat of the Red Sea was sapping his strength. By evening, he seemed to be in a delirium. From time to time, he would suddenly babble the English words Shinde had taught him at Port Said.

His mother and I spent that night in terror. But Shinde was resolute. The boy's babbling might wring his heart but it did not shake his nerve and he continued his treatment. From time to time, Louis's sweat would drench his linens and those would have to be changed. Liniment had to be rubbed on his limbs. He had to be fed milk at regular intervals. Fruit juice had to be made. Shinde would attend to all this himself. Louis's mother sat by the berth, her heart in her eyes. There were times when I feared for her reason. She kept asking Shinde questions as if to seek hope from him. And when he offered it, she rejected it as false assurance.

Shinde confided when she was out of earshot for a moment: 'I'm sure that I'll be able to save him. Children make good patients. They have no notion of death, no idea about what they'll have to leave behind or what they'll miss. That balances the lack of physical strength. Theirs is the power of the fearless heart.'

That day Herta and I barely met. When she heard about Louis, she came to my cabin and we managed to talk a little. She was ready to help with his care but Shinde forbade it. 'I don't even want his mother here but there's no helping that,' he explained. 'Too many cooks, you know. It just disrupts the patient's care.'

Aden arrived and with it Louis turned

the corner. His fever broke and he began to recognize people and feel hunger. He asked Shinde for coffee. Shinde's eyes filled with tears as he fed him some. Then he leaned his head on the bulkhead behind him, closed his eyes and almost immediately fell asleep—his first real sleep since Port Said.

Louis was carried back to his cabin. Later, when Shinde was leaning over the small form that was covered in a sheet, his mother hugged him and said, 'Doctor, you saved my child's life. And mine.'

That day an announcement: passengers to Shanghai had to be vaccinated against cholera and smallpox. Another announcement: passengers would have to pay for the injections, about a pound each, even in rupees. No one was sure whether this was truly needed but there was the fear that if you weren't inoculated, the authorities might refuse to let you disembark at Shanghai. Madnani saw his chance and worked on Marthe, exploiting her worries about money. Now he was taking full and public advantage of having her in his debt. His friends shared this pleasure too. All the Jews were aware of this.

Louis's mother began to see her predicament in a harsh new light. A sick child, no support, no money and an ordinary injection to be paid for in pounds? How would she pay for a serious illness? She began to think about what Marthe had done. Was she to lose her child or her self-respect?

We passed Aden and were now in the open sea. It was rainy weather and fierce storms were brewing. The ship began to roll and list in the heavy seas. High waves would often break over the deck, offering impromptu showers to those ill-advised enough to be sitting in deck chairs. It seemed as if the world were rocking on its axis. Almost everyone was affected by seasickness. It was difficult to walk straight. I had no appetite. If I stood up, I felt my stomach wobble. Everyone's innards were in the same parlous condition. The pain came and went but it left one in a state of collapse. My seasickness was compounded by a lack of sleep. A mild fever developed and I retreated to my cabin to rest and recuperate.

On the first day, Herta came and sat with me. On the second day, she was also sleeping. Shinde had been on his feet for two whole days but he too came and sat with me. Louis was well on the way to recovery, a thought that filled Shinde with satisfaction. He often talked about him. He came one evening when I was feeling a little better and was sitting up.

'Help me up on to the deck, will you?' I asked him. 'The fresh air might do me some good.'

'Two days in bed. Doctor's orders.'

'Two days, and we're in Mumbai,' I said.

'What's wrong with that?'

'I want to meet Herta.'

'Don't be silly,' Shinde said, shaking his head grimly. 'If there was any benefit from you falling ill, it's that you've been freed from that little entanglement.'

I ignored him and said, 'Doctor, I have to meet her. I want to meet her. Will you at least give her that message?'

'If you want. But I don't know whether she'll come. She spends all day on the deck as if she can't move or walk. Mannan is always hovering around, taking care of her, lavishing little attentions on her, whether she wants them or not. When night falls, he all but carries her below deck. I don't see how she will be able to get away and see you, even if she wants to.'

I could say nothing and collapsed back against the pillows.

'That's sensible,' Shinde mumbled.

~

Herta did come to see me around 9 p.m. She too seemed unsteady on her pins. Fatigue was obvious in every line of her body.

She put two apples down on the bed and said, 'The doctor says you're not eating. Try the apples. You'll feel better.'

My mind was filled with her defection. 'I don't feel like eating anything, Herta.'

'A little brandy then? It's good for seasickness.'

'Okay,' I said after a pause. 'I'll order it from the bar in a while.'

'Why pay for half a peg?' she asked and opened

her hankie. She had a small bottle concealed in it. 'I feel a little better after I've had a nip. Poor mother is surviving on aqua vitae.'

She offered the bottle to me. I got up and sat down. I was irritable now and said, 'Herta, you shouldn't even be here. Are you doing this just to annoy me?'

She did not get angry. In fact, she smiled a little. She pushed the bottle forward and said, 'Hmm. Down the hatch. Then I'll go.'

This excited me further. 'You know I can't bear these demonstrations of affection. Why bother? I can't stand it. You know that. This has to end. You know we can't marry.'

Helplessly, she put her head on my lap and said. 'How many times will you say it? I know that we can't marry. I have no hopes of it. But what do you get out of robbing me of the happiness of taking care of you? Of doing what I can while you're with me?'

I drank the brandy and sank back into bed. I did not want to think any more about this but willing a thought away is like trying to stop a stone from rolling down a mountainside and setting off an avalanche. I liked Herta. Very well, I loved Herta. But would it be wise to marry her? Love and marriage were two different things. A wedding was not the necessary outcome of love. It's the leavings of love, the crusts of bread at the end of a feast. I knew of various love marriages that had taken place in Maharashtra. They had all begun well and slowly the excitement had been drained out of them by the exigencies of daily living. Now only the ashes were left. I had also read various novels that featured love marriages. They all depicted how love blossoms and the burgeoning of it, all before marriage, of course. None of them dare to talk about what happens after marriage. They all end where they should begin.

I began to fear for myself. Friends who betray you can cause deep grief. If your business partner ditches you, you can come about, but what of a friend's betrayal? A lover's? When I had had no faith left in Uma, how could I trust Herta? And could I indeed consider myself worthy of expecting trust? There was just tomorrow and then Mumbai would spell the end. For a while we would remember and then the daily grind would take over. The business of living is a stone on which many griefs wear themselves out.

~

The ship had every facility you could reasonably expect, including a swimming pool but there were no calendars anywhere. You could never tell what day it was. Time was measured in ports that passed. As we touched shore, we would re-orient ourselves hurriedly. Otherwise the journey was spent in a tunnel of dark and light, star and sun...and everywhere the sea.

But today the crew was creating a commotion. Numbers had to be affixed on our luggage for the customs inspection. All the passengers were packing and suddenly clothes were turning up from the laundry necessitating the repacking of bags. You couldn't move in the barber's shop as on-board moustaches were being rethought. Bills were presented and debated, photographs were delivered. And memories were already being rehearsed and stored away.

Tomorrow, Mumbai.

But tomorrow meant twelve hours and everyone was in a hurry. Tomorrow yes, but tomorrow when? At what exact time? Everyone had an idea or was making a calculation. Distances were being measured. It was estimated that we would reach by the evening. A reprieve for me. A reprieve of twelve hours. I felt a little calmer.

As the ship approached the shores of Hindustan, the water seemed to get calmer too. The atmosphere had turned foggy, the sky dusty, the sea torpid. After three days of stormy seas, the five elements seem to have expended themselves and settled into a spell of calm.

Everyone was on the deck and for a change, all in one spot. The next day, at this time, they would all be scattered, perhaps never to meet again. We were all talking about the attractions of home: who was expected at the port, how many days they were going to stay, which trains they were going to take to travel further, when they expected to reach, how different things might seem after so much time had elapsed...

The Jews did not understand our language but our faces were so full of emotion, that there was no need for words. It all added up to the same song, with words that must have floated out and caught their ears: Mumbai, Hindustan; with the ever-present refrain: home, home, home. Most of the Indian passengers felt like prisoners on the last day of their jail term. The Jews were there for life.

The idea of photographs was first suggested by Shinde. It was he who got hold of a camera. I took a photograph of him and Louis. Then a rash of photograph demands broke out. Everyone wanted a shot of themselves with the people of their state; or with those who spoke the same language; or their cabin mates, table partners, whoever.

We were all standing on the deck. Keitel came along and said, 'I'd like photographs of all of you.' We got ourselves into position. Mannan, Herta and I were among the others. In that commotion, Herta whispered to me, 'Let's get a photograph taken of just you and me?' I nodded.

Mannan's friends were in front of us. They heard what she said. One of them said loudly, 'I'm taking some snapshots. Get together with Wifey.'

Herta shook her head. The man continued in Hindi, 'All day, all night, you're sitting together. Now you're acting coy about a couple of minutes.'

Mannan laughed and replied, 'Well, the lady won't play.'

'*Waah yaar*. Why won't she play? Are you a man or a mouse?'

'I've not hooked her yet. If we were married, I'd have shown her what's what,' he said and laughed again.

I was listening to all this. Herta was looking at the two of them. She did not know what they were saying. In my mind, a picture arose. A Jewish girl in love with a Hindu; a Muslim is drawn to her. If I married her, every meal she ate in my home would be alien corn. If she married him, she would have the same problems with the lifestyle and the food. At her age, she would be set in her ways. Her behaviour was different, her expectations too. Whatever home she found, she would have to work hard to adjust to the new atmosphere, the new habits and patterns of the family.

Herta refused again definitively. Mannan's friend looked at him and winked. He was suggesting that he take a candid shot, as if Herta were speaking to Mannan.

For a moment Mannan looked as if he were tempted. He put his arm around Herta's waist. She moved away. He came to his senses. Now he shrugged and said to his friend: 'Never mind. Don't force her.'

Herta dropped into an easy chair and said to me. 'What about our photograph? When do we take that?'

I was waiting for Shinde, I told her. Everyone was talking. Hermann said, 'The next twenty-four hours are going to be difficult for you.'

'Truly,' I replied but he meant one thing and I another.

Shinde came out on to the deck.

'Good news! There's a notice up on the first-class deck.'

Herta sat up with a start.

'Good news?'

'We reach Mumbai at 8 a.m. tomorrow.'

Her face went white.

'Tomorrow evening, right?'

'Tomorrow morning.'

I was standing by the rail. Shinde looked at me. I tossed my hat in the air.

'Hurrah! Joy in the morning.'

Herta went red with anger. She got up from her chair and stared at me. Her lips were a straight line of fury.

'Thank you very much for your eagerness.'

I too got a little excited.

'You're welcome, Fraulein.'

~

Sometimes a casually thrown stone can hurt a bird. From the pain in her voice, I could guess how much she had suffered. That voice came back to haunt me now. My mind was overcast. My excitement evaporated. I was really sorry. Even a cobra regrets the hurt it causes. I could not stay. I had been debilitated by seasickness and fatigue. Without looking at anyone, I turned to go to my cabin. Just as I set foot on the ladder, I heard Herta's voice.

'Bob, Bob, oh God.'

I was startled. I looked back. Herta's mother was lying in an easy chair at the edge of the storehouse. Her hair was white, her face lined with suffering, her body shrunken. She was seventy-five winters old, Herta had told me, and they showed. Herta was sitting at her feet. No, she had thrown herself on her mother's body. Now she buried her head in her mother's lap and was weeping. She did not even know I was near. She kept ducking her head and sobbing. I went close and called her name.

She looked up. God almighty, could this be Herta? Her eyes were blank, unseeing, all sparkle gone. Tears were gushing down her face. Her nostrils seemed to have collapsed, buds battered by a storm. Her mouth was askew. My heart sank. I tried to speak but no words came. Her lips remained closed too and when she tried to speak, her teeth stayed clenched.

She dropped her head again, burying her face in her mother's lap. I had no idea how to respond. Herta was seeking refuge from grief, looking in vain for what she had found in her mother's consolations as a girl. Her mother's hand was stroking her head but it was obvious from her face, that this was a weight too much for her to bear, even at the physical level. Herta was not aware of this; she took her mother's hand and brought it to her forehead, clung to her mother's wasted thighs, as if burrowing back into her mother's body, into the comfort and fearlessness of the womb. 'Mother,' she seemed to be saying without words, 'when you gave birth to me, I may or may not have wished to be born, I do not know. But take me back now into your womb. I cannot bear even the touch of the faintest breeze in this cruel world.'

~

Here was suffering then, the suffering of women that I had not believed in. 'If you could have seen what I was going through, you would have forgiven me,' Uma had written. Had she suffered? Perhaps she had. Had I known then, would I have been in a state to forgive her? Her rejection had been a blow but I had thought I had pieced myself together. And now this new blow, this new suffering. But what was it that Herta could not bear? Parting?

She had known that the relationship into which she was entering could not last and yet she had taken the plunge, had she not? Was it only out of some desire for experience, for intensity? Had it begun as an infatuation? Or was it just a matter of moonlight on the waves and enforced proximity? Had she thought that she would try to exchange one love for another, the pain of Karl for the pleasure of Bob? Had she imagined that she would try to retrieve hope only to discover despair?

I had seen her almost every day. By night, she would be in high spirits but by day her mood would turn grim. When she told me about Karl, I began to understand her a little better. That had been her first love. From her youth, she had internalized the high ideals of the Romantics; that had formed the basis of her love. Had her devotion fallen short of the ideal? Had she been found wanting? I knew that she was of a very good character.

That first love had come to naught and an even more terrible one had followed. That was what was unbearable to her. The cultural mores of her small country had shaped her values. She had believed that love is born once and dies once. But she had had to purge her mind of these beliefs and rely on her feminine instincts. The only problem was that when this had happened, her mind was no firm basis for love; it was quicksilver, it was lightning, sharp and terrifyingly bright. The brightness, the variability had been more than she could take. Was this what she had been feeling all these days? Had this been how she had looked at herself? Was this self now standing apart, repudiating her and the choices she had made? This was somewhat akin to what I had been feeling all these days, how I had thought of my self. Now where is that self? Does it stand apart to reject and humiliate me?

Even if all this were true, was it any help? Herta would think of Karl every day and her eyes would turn into stars. But stars have a tendency to fall out of the sky and turn to stone. Those stones rained down on her now, and had formed a tombstone. But beneath it, her mind was not dead, not yet, not blunted enough. A new love, a new life arose and with it, a new sky and a new storm. More wounds, further confusion.

I had to leave.

I left.

Two hours later, Herta came to my cabin. Shinde and Michael were with me. They were packing. I was lying on the top berth. She did not hesitate as she entered the cabin, nor did her demeanour reveal even a trace of hesitation. I was a bit startled. She had changed her clothes. She was now wearing a white silk dress. There was a corsage of pink flowers, and earrings in her ears. Her eyes were shining; happiness gleamed on her face.

She put her hand on my forehead and asked, 'What's this? Another fever?'

I got up and sat down. I took her hand in mine and said, 'Don't be silly. Just a little tired.'

'Oh no, you're not allowed that excuse. I'm going to revitalize you completely.'

Shinde said suddenly, 'Fraulein, may I remind you that there are impressionable young men present?'

'I fear no one and nothing,' she said with a laugh but she turned and went to the door and said, 'Bob. 9 p.m. On the deck?'

~

When it was 9, I was on the ladder to the deck. Herta met me there and insisted we go to the bar. She ordered beer. The steward brought us a bill. I was about to sign it when she stopped me and said, 'Hold on. I invited you. You are my guest.'

I said nothing. When the steward left, Herta asked: 'Annoyed?'

'I don't have the energy to be annoyed, but Herta you have behaved very badly with me.'

'Really? And how is that?'

'In eleven days, you've accepted nothing from me except for a couple of puffs from a stray cigarette. I've asked you so often but you've never had a drink with me. And now you're buying me a beer. Have you become suddenly very wealthy?'

She nodded vigorously.

'Very wealthy.'

I said savagely: 'As Marthe has?'

She looked at me angrily for a moment and then decided to forgive me. She pinched my arm and said, 'You've said that once. Don't say it again.'

After a silence, she said, 'Bob, you say I took nothing from you. But I took all that I wanted.'

The strains of the band invaded the bar. I pushed my chair back. One by one couples formed and drifted on to the dance floor. I watched the smoke rings form and float away lazily.

She stuck her chin out and said, 'Are you feeling lazy?'

I replied, 'Hm.'

She said, pretending anger: 'You're a liar.'

I said, as if to myself, 'True. I offered you hope and tomorrow...'

She protested immediately: 'Shut up. We're not to talk about that, right?'

I sighed.

'Very well but then why call me a liar?'

She pointed at the band.

'Do you recognize the tune?'

I pretended innocence and shrugged.

'No idea, m'dear.'

She tapped me on the cheek and said, 'Liar. That's a waltz. You know it's a Viennese Waltz. I also know you dance very well.'

~

It was she who plucked me from my chair and dragged me to the dance floor. She put my hand on her waist and tucked her fingers into my hand as one might tuck flowers into one's buttonhole.

And then her heels began to tap out the rhythm of the waltz and soon that too was almost lost in the sweetness of the music. The waves had taken up the rhythm. The melody deepened and mellowed. Many couples were now dancing, their bodies moving and swaying. Our steps grew lighter, our vision blurred, our bodies began to move as one. All sense of distance was erased. The dancers around us began to get more daring. The violins sang in tremolo.

At first Herta's face seemed confused, hesitant, a doll's face in porcelain expressing un-doll-like feelings. But then in the corner of her lips, a smile began to dawn. It was as if she were succumbing to the illusion that something would happen, something cataclysmic, that the ship might be wrecked and all on board would be drowned. These visions could not be sustained and they faded, and now we were on a fragrant river. All of us flowed with it, men and women, petals and leaves on the stream.

I suddenly remembered a story from my

childhood. In it, a handsome prince had gone fishing and when he cast his net into the sea, he found in it a beautiful woman. He took his sea-maid back with him to his palace. On the way, the cobwebs on a bush in a meadow caught the rays of the setting sun. To the sea-maid, they were the net in which she had been trapped and drawn from her natural environment. The fibres of the net had clung to her body. Each time one was raised, another would fall back against her. Their moist kisses had begun to defeat her. She could not tell the difference between the fact of the net and fictions of romance.

In the dark palace, she could hear the prince's voice in another room. A magnificent chandelier had been set in the ceiling of her room. His voice merged with the rainbow lights pouring down from the roof.

Her eyes were wet now, two blue lakes in which dreams came to roost, like a flock of thirsty birds. Here was rest, here was food and fresh water.

~

Once again, the frustration of the present broke through. We left the ballroom. Right in front of us, a clock. She looked at it and asked: 'Should I smash this? How it speeds!'

I stopped on the stairway: 'Which way do we go?'

'You choose,' she said.

I couldn't.

She said again, 'You're wasting time. Choose. Where do we go?'

I could not. Finally, she tired of my indecision and said, 'You're bored, aren't you? Very well. Back to your cabin and go beddy-byes.'

She turned. I could not understand the look she gave me.

'Herta,' I called.

'Yes,' she turned and now her face was eager.

'Nothing. Good night.'

'Yes indeed,' she said. 'Good night,' and then suddenly her face lightened again. 'I suddenly remembered when I said good night. In Switzerland when the radio programmes end, the hosts wish their listeners good night. You know how? "*Gute Nacht meine Damen, gute Nacht meine Herren. Schlafen Sie gut miteinander.*"'

I felt like laughing. The German had the intonation of a mantra.

'It sounds lovely but I have no idea what it means.'

'Let's go up on deck and I'll explain,' she said and set foot on the stairs. She stopped there and said, 'Oh dear. It's so hot.'

I replied. 'I'll stand on the deck. You jump into the water.'

She laughed. She ruffled my hair and pinched my cheeks and rested her head on my shoulder.

'Promise not to laugh.'

'What?'

'Let's go for a swim!'

~

The water in the swimming pool rocked with the movement of the ship. Its shimmering surfaces could not trap and hold the reflection of the night. I had put on my swimming trunks under my clothes; she had a blue swimsuit on too. I climbed on to the ladder. She let herself into the water first. Her body refracted in the water was a pale outline, rendered wavier and more indistinct by the movement of the ship, the movement of the water and her movements too. We began to play, refreshed by the coolness.

Somewhere in the middle of the pool, a plank had been placed crosswise. When I tired a little, I anchored my feet and began to float. She swam up to me and rested her head on my chest. Her eyes closed. Her hair brushed my cheeks and then she said, 'Shall we sleep like this all night?'

I laughed and said, 'Yes and die of pneumonia.'

'Let the morning take care of the morning. I am going to sleep like this. Good night, Bob, sleep well.'

That reminded me.

'You were going to tell me how Swiss radio says goodnight.'

'Oh yes. *Gute Nacht meine Damen* means "Good night, my ladies". *Gute Nacht meine Herren* means "Good night, my gentlemen". *Schlafen Sie gut miteinander* means...'

But then she held me a little tighter and said shyly, 'No, I don't think I can tell you, Bob.'

I made as if to push her away but she lost balance and went under. She came up again and found my legs first. Wet and shining in the dark, her hand reached for my neck. She hugged me.

I sought her mouth in the darkness and at last I managed to land a kiss on her lips. This was a reminder of other times spent like this.

~

At first, the lamp begins to glow. Then it emits light. Now the glass shatters, a breeze blows through the shards and calms the wick; then extinguishes it. But the candle flares before going out and has the satisfaction of those moments of burning brightly and peacefully. Herta broke through all the conventions with her uncontainable desire. She had released her energies in one great gust, once and for all. I could only stand outside and try to understand what was happening in this feminine vortex. This is how I imagined Herta in her cabin:

Herta climbs into her berth. All play has ended and yet the play has only begun. This was theatre, this was drama for one has to pretend a greater degree of intensity than one feels but this never satisfies anyone. For it is never possible to throw all restraint away and give oneself freely to the experience at hand.

She felt helpless, as if she were a tree, uprooted from the ground but required to remain upright. How long can one balance oneself without any support? How long before one keels over? Will support come before it is too late? Will tiredness claim one first? She had broken free in the gale of feeling, in the storm that was exile and was now being swept away.

Now there was nothing on her body but for a thin layer of cloth and the sheen of sweat. She was restless, unable to find peace within herself. When an aeroplane catches fire, the pilot bails out. He must take a leap of faith into the unknown, depending only upon his parachute to open and save him. Now his body falls, plunging to the earth, accelerating at the rate of ten metres per second squared. He pulls the ripcord and the parachute, silk butterfly, ersatz wings, billows out behind him, drawing him back from the pull of gravity.

The plunge is halted. Now another play begins as his body catches currents of air and rides the thermals. This may seem to last for an infinity but in its length is his salvation. Finally his feet touch the ground.

Karl's love had been like that. They had both played their parts in a socially-sanctioned piece of private theatre, a series of shy advances and coy retreats, gestures offered and accepted. This could all be contained by society.

What she was experiencing now was not like that. Everything was in a state of suspended animation and tomorrow there was going to be an earthquake so what of the ground beneath her feet?

Her heart turned to water.

Only six hours left.

When a calamity nears, it draws you towards it as the breath of a python is supposed to draw its prey to its mouth. Then one hurries towards the end, eager for consummation.

She covered herself. She wanted to sleep and forget about the morning. The past few days seemed as evanescent, as unreal as the light of a chandelier that is about to fall. She had fallen in love with those pretty colours and had allowed herself to be seduced by their rainbow promises. But now she realized that she was holding her breath, eager to hear the chandelier break and fall. Merciful darkness would follow but did she want the darkness of oblivion or the darkness of intoxication?

'Think. Think,' she told herself. 'Only ten days ago, a new world had emerged as if from the primeval ocean. In that world we lived and played. With such intensity we lived. Tomorrow that world will fall apart and "we" will end with it. To live again? And die again? Be ready for another death, this one caused by unsatisfied desires, so that the revenant will hover. I danced with him. When we swam, the water interposed and polluted our kisses.

'No, we had to extract the last drops of savour from the day. Destiny was pouring happiness on to us. I bathed in it to my heart's content. How can it be? I feel as if I have had nothing, as if I am still pining for it. The downpour continues and my thirst continues in parallel.

'Only six hours now.

'My lover is a call away. No, a whisper away. But why this distance that demands cries and whispers? Am I myself? Have I lost my senses, my sense of self?

'Still there is time. I will not leave his side for even a moment through every moment we have left. I will cling to his dark body as the moonlight and the water clung to him in the pool. His touch will destroy the mundane reality of flesh and blood and sinew.'

She sat up and threw the covers away. Her knees had been scraped. She looked at them now, examining them carefully to see how much they had been hurt. There was a little blood. To see it better, she turned on the light and then turned it off again almost immediately. For she realized in that instant that she had no clothes on. How could she go to his cabin in that state?

'Such quandaries. Such restrictions. We seem hedged in by them even in this new-made floating world. One might want to think about them now but where was the time to think? The advance and retreat of the waves mock our short-lived world. The clock's hands race on. The hour of parting is rushing towards us and we are trapped. The shore of happiness is in front of us but our hands are tied, our mouths gagged. It has ever been thus. On Berlin Station, Karl had been so close but the Gestapo had kept us apart. The ship had docked at Port Said and landfall had been a metaphoric short step away, the Holy Land of Palestine, no less, but I was not allowed to disembark. The cliché re-enacts itself again and again: so near yet so far. No different today.'

She shook herself. It was as if she had

broken some chains that had been holding her back. The illusion grew stronger. A small cabin, its air cool, dark, it had taken on the feel of a prison. In front a porthole; outside the waves at play. For a moment, she became aware of another reality. She understood what she had done. She had cast off her fetters and jumped from the porthole. Free at last, free to pursue happiness...

Looking at her mother in the berth beneath, Herta's courage failed her. Standing there, she laid her head on the bedclothes. She began to dream.

*She had been arrested. She was in the dock. In the seat of justice was Thought. He called on the accused in a harsh, angry voice.*

*She did not raise her head.*

*It was you who jumped out of the window of the prison, was it not?*

*Yes, milord.*

*Did you not see how high the window was?*

*No, milord. I could see nothing of the outside world from my cell.*

*And the water in the moat? Were you not afraid of that?*

*I saw the fish swimming in the water, how they broke the surface for a moment and then went down again. I thought: fear is futile.*

*To prevent you from fleeing, there were guards posted.*

*Light would fall on them. They seemed to point the way to freedom. They were calling me outside.*

*For a moment, silence fell. She trembled in anticipation of her sentence. Once again he called upon her.*

*She did not raise her head.*

*'Go, you are free.'*

She did not wait. She raised her head. She put on her sandals and covered her body. Without thinking, she opened the door and came out.

Her mother was fast asleep. She turned over now and gave a sigh. Was it relief? Was it protest? Or satisfaction that Herta had made some decision? Or a blessing from a woman who had lost the courage required of motherhood?

When Herta stepped in, I was still awake. No one else was in the cabin but had there been someone, I do not think it would have turned her from her purpose.

I was startled but all I could say was: 'Herta?'

'Yes. Me. I left that translation incomplete, didn't I? I came to tell you what it meant.'

She was leaning on the clothes cupboard. I found no words. Staring at me, she added.

'*Schlafen Sie gut miteinander*. Do you know what it means? Sleep well with one another.'

Once the words were out, she bit her lips. She was moving so fast it was as if she could not slow down for fear of falling. She put her hand on the looking-glass behind her. Her gaze did not falter.

After a while she said, 'Nothing to say, Bob?'

She seemed to be awake but not in her senses.

In a slightly frightened voice, I said, 'Herta, what are you up to?'

She stood her ground. She took hold of my arm and said, 'Still trying to save me from myself, Bob? I know what you'll say. This is not a good thing you're doing. What will people say?

Which people are you talking about, my dear? The Germans? The Egyptians? The Indians? None of them have room for me. You have a world waiting for you, with its friends and its moralities. I am a non-person to them. I have no people, so whose morality do I follow? If I had four walls to call my own, a home, I could put on some clothes. I could hide my shame. But when a storm is raging about your head, does it matter how you're dressed? The wind buffets you, the waves make play with you, your bones become brittle and will only shred your clothes. Once again, you will be naked and once again you will be sending out the same moral message.'

But then she stopped completely. She realized that before she expended her energy, she should take the plunge. Her intensity was uncontrollable. Her neck, her shoulder, every part of her body was shivering. She held herself and said, 'I came to ask a favour, Bob. Your eyes have seen my body like this...'

But she could not finish what she was saying. She had only draped a dressing gown over her shoulders. Now she dropped it to the floor in a quick, decisive gesture. She stood there, brave and beautiful, with all the natural grace of a stalk of corn, just out of its husk.

Her gaze dropped. Her head drooped. She turned her back on me. Her hands fell to her sides. 'Oh God,' she said in a voice full of pain.

The curtain was blowing in the breeze. After I locked the door, it stopped. There she was still, her unclothed body caught in the relentless gaze of the mirror. The storm continued to rage.

~

Only a very little light fell on the berth. The slanting rays turned her body to gold. My gaze lingered on her. Such moments make you into a painter: only the colour, the line, the shadow, the light holds your attention. Then you begin to wonder: is it an image or a body? No, it could only be a painting but one made today or in the past? A painting made today would be composed of the play of light and shade but then that transferred light had a certain sharpness and intensity. Half her body was in shadow, as if in surrender; it was full of warmth and pain. Could it be a picture in the present? If it were a picture in the past, it becomes simple. There's no made-up beauty, no colour splashed around. A simple frame like a mirror, the background of glass and a marble image. No, it was neither of the present nor of the past. It was the personification of every woman of every moment, in the act of offering. Her wet hair clung to her head. A single lock had strayed on to her forehead, where it formed a question mark. How intoxicating this challenge of intense love. The necklace was shimmering. Her hair was a flame to which a moth might be drawn. From her navel, a line of hair ran down into a bower of flowers. It gave my bloodlust the power of sight.

~

There was no novelty in a woman's body for me. I thought back over the past two years. I am telling you the truth now with God as my witness. Each night in London, I would stroll down the streets near Piccadilly. I would sit in a café or hang around the glass doors of shops. In those milling crowds, I could always pick out the prostitutes. They were good at eluding the police who were always in pursuit. As I was.

I never used the same woman twice. Many foreigners do the same for fear that the girl might form an attachment. That was not my reason. I was afraid that *I* might fall in love with one of them. Yes, I felt disgust for them too. Is it possible to love what disgusts you? Why not, if it is possible to be disgusted often by what you love?

But why talk of those two years? I remember the nights in Paris: the dance halls, the theatres, the cabarets, the restaurants. At each of these places, I could watch women exhibiting their flesh. Eventually, with four Indian friends, I went to a brothel. A large drawing-room lit by dim blue-green lights. At the windows, on the ceiling, on the tables, everywhere mirrors. In the middle of this, fifty or seventy-five prostitutes, their naked bodies reflected and multiplied in those mirrors. A river of alcohol was flowing. But that was not the only intoxicant. There was another concocted of lust and desire, more potent because it was imaginary. It flowed freely, incontinently from the ceilings, down the walls, over the floors.

The Hindu numeral three—and its Roman variant—is considered the most beautiful of designs or shapes in the configuration of figures. In terms of the flesh, it is the body of a woman. But I was disgusted by those sinuous snake shapes. It was as if the female bodies were made tumescent by the lustful gaze of men. It was unbearable to watch them if you had not given in to the seduction of the moment. The women were scratching their bodies, their hair. To blot out their degradation, to blur it a little, it was necessary to drink.

I came out of the salon. Our guide was French. I gave him a cigarette and asked, 'Henri, is this what the beauty of women amounts to?'

He laughed and replied, 'Monsieur, if those women were dressed and crossed your path, you would have turned to look at them.'

'Do men come here in the hope of being excited?'

He blew a smoke ring and said, 'For the same reasons you came.'

'I turned away. Do others turn away too?'

'If they have retained some humanity. If they have been drinking and so have turned themselves into animals, no.'

I was surprised by his tone.

'You're a guide, Henri.'

'So?'

'Why such disgust?'

He shook his head.

'If you come here Monsieur and you look at these women, you begin to be repulsed. You feel disgust for women. What a race! I can't believe I was born of one.'

I turned back to look again into the house. From the door, one could see them coquetting and flirting. They looked like female serpents in a glass showcase, repulsive, but you could not look away.

~

You can see that I was too experienced to be excited by Herta's nakedness. What could be new in a body? The same flesh, the same blood, and yet each time, these change and reveal new designs, as if a cosmic garden should have a million pots and in each pot a new plant. And yet, here she was in a state of abject surrender. It was not possible to control myself.

It seemed as if the moment would overcome her, as if she might faint from the intensity of her feelings. She slumped over the cupboard. I got up and lifted her and set her down in the berth. She curled up like an infant.

# Six

What follows were written on the ship's letterhead. In the order in which they arrived. The translations are my own.

***Between Mumbai and Colombo***

***September 1939***

So you did disembark, Bob? Did you leave nothing of yourself behind?

You left and the old pain returned. Herr Keitel has packed his notebooks away. His enthusiasm for English seems to have waned considerably. He says that Mr Vidhwans was a fine teacher of English.

Do you remember Auchapal? There was an Anglo-Indian girl with you. You were a bit contemptuous of her flirtatious behaviour and yet it was by her example that you first took me in your arms. Auchapal and she were not behaving badly. They have decided to get married.

But she has left and now Auchapal sits in the bar, talking to no one, drinking steadily. Do you remember Louis? The uncle who cured him of his Anglophobia has also abandoned him. Now he says suddenly to his mother, 'Mutti, I like English very much' and 'Mutti, come on say, "Ah, you're a sweet chap".' When I think of Dr Shinde, I feel terrible. With us, there were always underlying expectations that contaminated our love. Our love made us a bit selfish. He was not selfish in his affection. The night we spent together, engrossed in each other, he told Louis's mother that he wanted to adopt the child. She refused to give up her child and so he offered to take on both of them. They spent the day trying various stratagems. But it was all in vain. They were given the same reply that you were.

From *The Times*, the headlines surrounded by a black box: Britain at war with Germany. The obituary of our dreams, Bob.

As German passport-holders, we were seen as German citizens, enemy aliens. Hindustan was close to us but so far away. Bob, yesterday, we were all friends. Today, we are enemies. For ten days, we played at love on the high seas. Today, the world is a war zone. The war has begun in Europe. I am free of Germany but have I been freed from war or have I been tossed into the middle of it? Had I been in Germany, I might have been caught in an air-raid and died. But I would have died just once. Now because of our separation, I must die again and again.

Are we truly enemies? Not so long ago, we were strangers. Then we were friends. Now enemies. In the face of our love, this is illogical, unimaginable. You are a subject citizen of the British empire. I have lost my German citizenship. We are both exiles. And yet we are enemies.

But it is true that I am a German. I will continue to be one. My heart breaks. Those beautiful meadows of my memories will soon we reduced to ashes. The trees in the forests will find it hard to understand why they are being devastated before winter comes. The beautiful sky over Germany will rumble with the roar of bombs. The ground will shiver in fear.

What should we do? The Nazis maintain that the Jews are traitors. Some Jews on board were saying that if they were given a chance they would join the British army to fight the Nazis.

In other words, Bob, these were Germans saying they wanted to fight Germany. Does that make them traitors? Would we seek a victory for Germany? Would a victory for Germany be a victory for Nazism? Or would it be the victory of a pogrom? Would it be the victory for democracy? Or for a political philosophy that would corrupt the notion of democracy? Germany's loss means my nation's defeat.

At such times, one feels that if workers are pushed too far, tortured too much, exploited too long, they will revolt. The Communists want this to happen. They expect this to happen. Perhaps the boundaries of narrow patriotism need to be broken all over the world. If the Nazi philosophy spreads, minorities in every country will be tortured. They will be ruined. The next generation will not know where they belong. The world will begin to belong to those who believe that in numbers lie strength, that might is right.

My mother was born in Poland. I was born in Berlin. My children, should I have any, will be born in Shanghai. When your grandmother is Polish and your mother is German and you are Chinese, for whom will you fight?

But even to achieve that distant dream, Hitler must not win today. So I must resign myself to hoping that my country loses for I do not wish it to carry the burden of blame for all the atrocities that must follow.

Personally I believe that as women we must fight all the Hitlers who begin wars, of every nation and every political philosophy. That is our right. For a culture of war is a culture that hates women. Two wars in one generation! The glory of the nations seems to depend now on how powerful they are in war and destruction and the killing of people. This is not what women understand as glory. Our glory lies in creation. It is based on our ability to give birth to a new generation. Louis has lost the loving care of Dr Shinde. Your children and mine and those of Auchapal will remain unborn.

I, Louis's mother, that Anglo-Indian girl, we would all have been united in our opposition to war. Why should it be improbable that those who are about to lose their fathers, brothers, lovers, husbands, sons should get together to fight?

Bob, do you think I would be accepted were I to apply to the British Army?

Herta

## *Colombo-Singapore*

Till yesterday, I felt the whole world was in a furnace. How then can one's personal joys and sorrows matter? But the pain is sharp if a wound is fresh. I wrote about our love marriage. Now it is difficult to believe it.

At dawn, you woke up and brought me to the deck and said, 'Herta, I am going to marry you.'

I was exalted to the heavens. I began to dream of coming back from Shanghai. I could not believe my ears. For a while, my happiness filled the world and threatened to spill over.

Bob, on the first day that you drew me close, you regretted it almost immediately. You said, 'Herta, this affair can have no proper ending. I would never be able to marry you.'

And that was when I told you that I would make do with the joy of so paltry a thing as a shipboard romance. My life had become a long dark night with no dawn in sight. Your love was like a lamp burning in the darkness. I would take what light and warmth I could get from it. I would be content with that much. No, I would be happy with that much.

So what happened that morning? What changed your mind? What made you ready to marry me? I know the principles you like to live by. You believe that women hunt men for marriage. When all other tricks fail, they spread their love traps for men.

Then when men behave badly, they try to

make them feel guilty. For a guilty man will do anything he can to ease his shame. He submits to his fate.

That was it, wasn't it?

When you left, you apologized. What did you think you had done that you had to ask my forgiveness? You tried your best to turn me away when I offered myself to you. So what were you expiating when you offered marriage?

In Berlin, my loneliness was insuperable. I would play chess against myself, an empty chair in front of me, and often I would lose. The game we played was similar in its one-sidedness, wasn't it?

I forced you to play. I could see you had some experience with women. I could also see that you pretended a disgust of my sex. But what I felt for you overcame all that. Against your wishes, I drew you in.

But if you felt no love for me, whence came that offer of marriage, Bob? Was it just a matter of pity?

I did not want pity, Bob. I do not need

refuge. Mannan was offering marriage right up to the end. He could not bear you. Nor could he bear to see our attraction for each other. He kept painting pretty pictures of the happy times I would have if I married him. But I could feel no anger at all this, only boredom. That was why I turned him down.

Who knows what I would have done had I not met you? He seemed to have a loving nature and a huge ambition. He took good care of my mother and of me, after Aden. One day, I was so seasick that my head was filled with a haze. He brought me some fruit and was insisting that I eat it. I said, 'I don't want fruit, Bob dear. Bring me some brandy.'

He did not get angry that I had called him Bob. Nor did he stop looking after me. How much can one man take? He came to our cabin to say farewell. He wanted to speak to my mother who had no English and so he said to me, 'Fraulein, I must ask you to promise that you will translate into German whatever I am going to say.' I had no idea what he was going to say but I promised anyway.

Mutti was looking at him. He was choking with tears as he began. 'Mother, I have no parents. I am an orphan but I come from good stock. I love your daughter very much. May I tell you how much? Please tell her to marry me so that you can be my mother too.'

I broke down. He was weeping too. I could say nothing. Mother was confused. We went to dance. Just before that I had had a little argument with her.

Mannan's dreams were all about the victory of Islam. One day Hindustan would no longer be Hindu and he was awaiting that day with much impatience. If I had married him, I would have had to teach my children to hate your children.

But what of that? I did meet you. And I will live for long on the memory of those ten days.

Herta

***Singapore-Manila***

Enough.

Bob, I want you. But I am to have none of you. I understand this now and I am done for.

I should be punished. I am a sinner. I am a criminal. Who you are, I do not know. You came and you went. I loved you and I lost all sense of shame. I was not worried about the opinions of others, not even of my own opinion of myself. I seem to have fallen out of love with Karl. What should be my sentence? I should like to hear it pronounced.

May they forgive me, my comfortably settled sisters, who would be the jury of my peers. You poor things, you're lucky. Your love and commitment are steady. Your devotion does not get corrupted by outside influences. Your dedication is ceaseless. I am one of you, a woman too. So how could I do this?

But caught up in calamity, I seemed to be helpless. It is as if a tree collapses and a creeper remains.

I uprooted myself. We women may seem to be flighty but really we're not. We are alert and our motives are often selfish. We do not surrender ourselves until we gauge the person to whom we are going to surrender.

I remember being attracted very often to men after I came of age. There was a tobacconist's in front of our home. The boy who worked there had an incredibly sweet smile. But he ruined it all when he opened his mouth to speak. There was a doctor, later, a doctor who made house-calls. He was stout and solemn and very good at his work. He seemed powerful but he was not sensitive.

One day, there was a new professor at our college. He was handsome, intelligent and learned too. But he seemed to have no idea of what the world was like outside the covers of a book.

I did my share of playing, wandering, roaming, dancing. I was a bee, flirting with flowers, but looking for a wooden beam to make my nest. Then I met Karl. I liked so much about him: his grace, his manners, the intensity of his speech, his sense of himself. He had a sharp tongue but there was freedom in his laughter. He was intelligent even if he wasn't learned. He was powerful too and in his arms I lost myself and forgot about the future.

Then came the apocalypse.

Our homes were destroyed. Our dreams were ground to dust. We became accustomed to contempt, mistreatment, disrespect. We got used to being targets. Now I was driven from the gardens of delight that I had thought of as my birthright. I was forced to hide. My home turned into a prison. And slowly one forgot that one was a prisoner. For one was terrified of the freedom that the world represented.

That was my state when I came on board. There you were playing cards in the bar. Your laugh rang out, free, easy. It drew my attention to you because it brought the walls of my Jericho tumbling down.

And then our eyes met. I was ready for you at that very moment. My heart, I remember, was pounding with joy.

It has often occurred to me that women do not love men. We call our instincts love and this is what we love, our expectations, our hopes. Where we see the chance of those hopes turning into reality is where we turn our attention.

When one loses something, one's mind seeks a similar object or person and will not rest until it has found a substitute. This is what probably accounts for our fascination with the afterlife. Is this why séances are popular, why the bereaved seek mediums? One can get lost in this alternative to reality. Love is like that. When it perceives a way to survive, it will grab that chance. Is this deception?

That was how you first drew my attention. You had something of Karl's grace in you. When I saw you, your clothes were in charming disarray but there was a carefree quality to that too. It offered an insight into your personality. Your laugh reminded me of his. Your speech seemed to be full of fire. Mannan was persuasive but you played the game of love as if it were a war. You retreat but only after you have drawn blood.

My dear, my heart was an ill-used and misbegotten thing after its share of the briars of the cruel world. You accepted it as if was. Christ turned the water into wine with a single glance. Your acceptance performed a similar alchemical transformation in mine. In your stern gaze I could see a trace of affection. I would find myself looking for it, again and again. However much your adamantine surfaces hurt me as I threw myself against them, however much it cost me, I would keep on trying until I simply surrendered and found a hidden gentleness in you. You built a beautiful world of words and I found myself a home there.

This was the love that I tried to grab with both hands, hands that proved too weak to hold on to it.

I want you, Bob.

But I cannot have you.

I am done for.

ALSO IN SPEAKING TIGER IN ASSOCIATION WITH JSW AND INDIAN NOVELS COLLECTIVE

## FIFTY-FIVE PILLARS, RED WALLS: PACHPAN KHAMBE, LAAL DEEWAREIN

Usha Priyamvada

Translated from the Hindi by Daisy Rockwell

First published in 1961, Usha Priyamvada's debut novel *Pachpan Khambe, Laal Deewaarein* is located within the boundaries of an all-women's college in Delhi. Behind its walls is Sushma Sharma—lecturer, warden, single, and sole provider for her large family. Despite her relative youth and elegance, she is resigned to the regimented loneliness of her life, until a chance meeting with the charismatic Neel. Then, long-thwarted desires uncurl and the shackles she has accepted suddenly begin to seem unbearable. But the world around her is still unchanged, and independence still causes scandal...

In spare, evocative prose, *Fifty-five Pillars, Red Walls* skilfully explores the physical, mental and social paradigms which locked so many women into narrow ideals, as they still do. Daisy Rockwell's pitch-perfect translation brings this quietly intense, poignant and pathbreaking Hindi novel into the blazing spotlight of classic Indian literature for the first time.

ALSO IN SPEAKING TIGER

## FRAGMENTS OF HAPPINESS

Shrilal Shukla

Translated from the Hindi by Niyati Bafna

When Durgadas, an ordinary businessman from Delhi, is arrested for murder in Lucknow, the lives of the people he left behind—his family and friends— unravel in unexpected ways. As they fight to prove his innocence and deal with the upheaval in their lives, they find themselves turning against each other. Taranath, his eldest son, searches for meaning and strength in religion and ritual when the law seems to fail him. Rajnath, his younger son, finds his marriage with his wife, Neela, coming undone when they decide against having a child until Durgadas is acquitted. His youngest daughter, Chaand, struggles with her attraction towards Vimal, the much older family friend and Durgadas's confidant. Vimal's integrity and Chaand's loyalties are tested as people around them try to drive them apart.

*Fragments of Happiness* follows the tumult of ordinary people learning about their own power and helplessness in the face of extraordinary circumstances. Originally published in Hindi in 1973 as *Seemayein Tootati Hain*—five years after the cult classic *Raag Darbari*—with this novel Shrilal Shukla proves himself to be as great a master of tragedy as he was of satire.